The Sensitives

The House of Here, Volume 2

D.A. Riles

Published by D.A. Riles, 2025.

This is a work of fiction. Similarities to real people, places, or events are entirely coincidental.

THE SENSITIVES

First edition. February 8, 2025.

Copyright © 2025 D.A. Riles.

ISBN: 979-8230165415

Written by D.A. Riles.

Also by D.A. Riles

The House of Here
The Sensitives

Standalone
The Monster We Call Dad
The House of Here

Table of Contents

The Sensitives | Epilogue 1
The End ... or is it just the beginning? 119

I am grateful for all the support given to me from my family.

Emily, Asher, and Jacob planted their seeds in our birth parents. For we are the ones who must complete this coming mission. This is the beginning of a new age, an age of turmoil and enlightenment."

The Sensitives
Epilogue

"We are singular, yet connected by Time. He has linked us all into one. We are the Sensitives!

We are from Earth, but our creation is different than most. Our mother is Emily and our fathers' are Jacob and Asher. Though we have been in many other females' wombs, Emily is our birth mother, for it is her eggs that have been planted in us. We are the creation of the sun, the moon, and nature. We have been created for the betterment of humanity. We have knowledge of much, but not of everything.

Emily, Asher, and Jacob planted their seeds in our birth parents. For we are the ones who must complete this coming mission. This is the beginning of a new age, an age of turmoil and enlightenment."

Chapter One

"Mom! Mom!" Zenny screamed as she hopped out of bed from her brief nap. Running into the kitchen where her mother was putting away the dishes, she said excitedly, "Mom! They came to me again. This time they were telling me about where they are from and how they were made."

"Oh, stop it Zen'obia, you and your dreams are just that! Dreams! Stop bothering me and stop pretending that other beings come and talk to you. You're too old for that. You're twenty-three! When are you going to grow up?" Mom said with exasperation.

"But Mom," Zenny pleaded, "they *are* real and they *do* talk to me!"

Mom turned on her heel and walked out of the room. Shaking her head at her daughter's incessant admissions to hearing other worldly beings, the elderly woman no longer wanted to hear such nonsense.

Seeing her mom's back as she left the kitchen, Zenny said quietly with a childish pout on her lips, "They do exist, and they are real."

Walking back to her bedroom, Zenny sat on the edge of the bed and cupped her face in her hands thinking, *"Why does Mom refuse to believe me? This has been happening all my life, as far back as I can remember and yet, she still doesn't believe me. I even told her things that were about to happen and I proved that I knew it ahead of time, but still she refutes it. Why does she refuse to believe me!"* Feeling her mother's disapproval of her gift, Zenny contemplated her life. *"I'm so tired of trying to prove that the things I see and hear are real,"* Zenny continued to pout. *"I know there is more to this life than what I've been taught!"*

Chapter Two

Several days later, Zenny was walking home from work with a co-worker.

"Zenny," Jessica said in a questioning tone, "I've noticed that you've been unusually quiet these last several days; what's going on?"

"Nothing," Zenny replied a bit too quickly, as they continued their walk.

"I know you better than that. We've been friends from nearly the day you started working at the WebNet, and that's been over four years ago. So just tell me, what's going on?"

Deciding to tell her friend a little bit about it, hoping that she would get some form of help from her, Zenny replied, "Oh, you know … it's my mom, she just doesn't have the same belief system that I have and sometimes it gets hard being at home with her," Zenny said as they continued their two mile walk back to their homes.

"What is your belief system?" Jessica questioned with real interest.

"Well, you know how at times, I know when things are about to happen? Well it has to do with that," Zenny replied.

"Is it really such a big deal that your mom doesn't believe you?" Jessica questioned not understanding why it suddenly mattered now, especially since it's been that way for all of Zenny's life.

"I know that it didn't bother me much before, but lately it's been very difficult wanting to be in the same room with her, for she just shuts me out, before she will even listen to me. I like talking about the things that I know, especially when I know of things to come. I like bringing up the things I know," Zenny continued on more to herself, than to Jessica. "It's hard for me to talk to her without me wanting to bring things up that I've found out or dreamed about. I find them to be so interesting," Zenny said with sorrow in her voice.

"I understand what you're saying, but your mom might not like knowing about the future and what is or might happen. For some people it scares them. I've never been that way, for I find it intriguing and interesting." Thinking for only a moment, Jessica added, "What about moving out and into your own place?"

"I've tried. I've been looking for any open housing, but there is none around that is within walking distance for me. And since the iron is becoming scarce and other materials are running out, the cost of a moving machine is out of the question."

Interjecting, Jessica commented, "We're neighbors and co-workers. We live only one house apart." Taking in a deep breath to gain courage, Jessica blurted, "What if we find a place together? That would save us both a lot of money, and perhaps we could afford to rent a moving machine, or even take the Levotrain and ride in it together. I know some of our neighbors take the Levotrain and they say it's not that bad, as long as you don't mind sitting next to someone else." Perking up, Jessica added, "we could always try to get seats next to each other. We wouldn't have to leave so early for work, and we wouldn't get home so late either."

"It does sound like a good idea, and maybe I wouldn't have to pay as much rent as I do with living with my mom," Zenny said with a bit of excitement in her voice.

Chapter Three

Weeks later the two women had found a place that they both could afford, even though it was farther from work. Taking the Levotrain made the distance unimportant, for they still left for work later than when they use to walk to work and they arrive home sooner.

Things were going very well between the two friends. Jessica had male callers, while Zenny kept to herself. She wasn't ready to let someone into her life and expose them to the disturbing reality of her dreams.

Jessica had noticed some of the strangeness that her friend had been talking about. She would notice that things would move from their place without the help of a person moving it. She was told by Zenny where not to go if she felt that something bad might happen. In the beginning Jessica didn't take her seriously, but it didn't take long for Jessica to find out that if Zenny said don't go to a certain place; she shouldn't go.

One night when Jessica was preparing for a date, Zenny said, "I really wish you would reconsider going. I told you what would happen, please don't go," she begged her friend.

"Oh Zenny don't worry, I'm not going to get hurt," Jessica replied. "I will be extra careful tonight, okay?"

Shaking her head Zenny watched as her friend left their home with her date. Two hours later Zenny received a call, it was Jessica.

"Jessica, are you alright?" Zenny questioned with fear in her voice.

"Everything is okay, but I won't be coming home for a few days. We're in the hospital. Keen has a few broken ribs and I broke my wrist and leg, but we will be fine." Trying to cover her apprehension, Jessica added, "We were driving and the other car came out of nowhere and T-boned us. It was totally his fault. The other driver is fine." Silence fell upon their conversation, then Jessica said, "I'm sorry I didn't believe you. You know it's just hard to accept such things," she said sheepishly.

"That's alright," Zenny said, then added, "I'm happy that you and Keen will be fine. Are you going to let WebNet know that you won't be into work for a while, or would you like me to tell them?"

"I'll call them so they will be able to see that I am actually at the hospital, that way they won't dispute my time off. Thanks for asking," Jessica said sincerely.

After that incident, Jessica never questioned Zenny again.

Chapter Four

Three months had passed and Zenny hadn't had any dreams of the strange woman who would tell her things. Life was going well and things were running smoothly, but then one night ....

"Soon those with eyes to see and those with ears to hear, will know who and what we are. But, for now we hide ourselves as we try to do what we can to prevent the complete destruction of the Earth. Our planet is out of alignment, but most are unaware of its displacement.

Looking up to the moon, it is still where it should be? Is its face tilted in the wrong direction? What about the crescent of the moon? Does it look like a right bracket) or a left bracket (or does it look like the lips on a 'smiley face'? Observe it for many months and capture its rotation at night. Does it look normal to you? Are seafaring vessels still able to reliably use the moon as a navigational tool, or has something changed? Is the sun still rising in its proper place in the East? Is it off a few degrees? What about the magnetic North? Is it migrating further North heading to the largest underwater volcano?"

Zenny's body quivered in her sleep as the dream continued on.

"We are grown now and ready to fight for humanity. We want to help those who are also willing to fight and survive, but not many will hear our words. If you are ready to help us in our time of need we will be waiting for you."

Chapter Five

The following morning, Zenny woke up after a very restless night. She remembered quite well what was told to her, but was uncertain as to how she would be able to meet up with these beings, for she had no way of contacting them. Zenny was willing to do all she could to save as many people as possible, for she knew that the things she had been told were true. She could feel it permeate through her youthful body.

After the two women arrived home from work, Zenny said, "I would like to talk to you about a dream I had ... if you don't mind."

"Is it about me? Is something bad going to happen to me?" Jessica queried.

"Well," Zenny hesitated, then said, "It's about the world."

Jessica was silent as she walked over to their living room couch and sat down. Zenny followed and sat on the couch next to her friend. Placing her hands in her lap, she grasped them together, as she waited for Jessica's reply.

"From the tone of your voice," Jessica said finally said as she broke the long silence, "I can tell it's not something good. Can I have some time to think about it?" she questioned.

"How much time were you thinking?"

"Oh great, that makes me even more worried when your asking for a time line," Jessica responded with honesty and fear in her voice.

"I'm sorry, but it really does have a limitation on time," Zenny replied as she lowered her head.

"Is tomorrow to late?"

"No, I think that will be okay," replied Zenny.

Later that night, after the two had finished supper, Jessica said, "It's a hard question to answer. I don't know if I want to know what is going on."

"I understand completely," Zenny replied. "I've lived my whole life with people not wanting to know what was going to happen to them. Most people are afraid of the truth. They would rather be told lies. They prefer to believe the things the higher ups tell people on the WebNet, than what they can see with their own eyes, if they would just look," Zenny commented openly.

"I will give you my answer in the morning. Is that alright?" Jessica questioned.

"It's fine with me. But, don't think you have to say yes just to appease me," Zenny said as she gave her friend's shoulder a light squeeze with a smile as she stood. "I'm going to get a snack and then head off to bed. Are you going out tonight?"

"No, I'm staying in. I've had enough of Keen and his constant bragging," Jessica replied with a smile as she watched her friend walk over to the kitchen.

Chapter Six

Zenny opened her bedroom window to let the cool summer night air into the room. Feeling a soft breeze brush over her body, she finished readying herself for bed. Flinging the sheets back from her bed, she crawled in and lay her head upon the feather pillow. The night air felt good against her body, peacefully she drifted off to sleep.

"Only a few will survive what is about to come. But, most won't even know anything is happening until it is much too late to prepare. The few who are preparing are ridiculed, teased, taunted, called scare-mongers, and many are simply dismissed by those who are supposed to love and support them. But, the chosen will continue to prepare no matter what hurdles are thrown at them, for they know that the time of destruction is imminent. Open your heart, let Time speak with you. Let Him guide you to do what is right. Turn away from negativity, media lies, and the rulers who are trying to Control *you. Turn your heart to light and love. Allow yourself to be who you are and not who others want you to be. Though innumerable souls will be taken to the dark, some will follow the light and for those who do, they ought to give thanks to Time for all He has done for them. Most souls won't live through what is about to come. But saving the human soul is possible through judgment, only if they partake in the healing of love and kindness before they pass into the void of the non-living. Tell the people that their moral depravity, social injustices, mass genocides, and numerous criminal and sadistic acts are*

consistently monitored by the Prayer Pickers and Time. For those who will heed the warnings, tell them to immediately stop watching "programs" for that is just what they are... PROGRAMS, they are made to influence the vulnerable and keep their minds occupied with rubbish!"

"This is very disturbing," Zenny muttered in her sleep as her dream continued on.

"Do not fear child, for I will be there to guide you to do what is right and what must be done. I will be there to help you prepare for what is to come. Whether your fate is to perish or to persist; I will guide you as best as I can. When we meet, you will see that we are much alike, for I am just like you, but I have the ability to communicate with the sleeping. I was taught this as a young child, and I will teach you how to reach willing souls. They are waiting for aide from us. They are lost and in need of guidance and love."

Chapter Seven

"Zenny, wake up!" Jessica yelled as the wind howled loudly outside.

Waking with a jolt and a shiver running through her body, Zenny noticed her curtains flailing about as the wind whipped through her room. The air was frigid.

"What's going on?" Zenny questioned, not understanding what happened to the cool night air.

"I don't know," shouted Jessica trying to make her voice heard through the howling of the wind. Moving over to the open window Jessica swiftly shut the offending window as she continued in a loud, but not shouting voice. "I woke up to the sound of the wind and the freezing air. I don't understand how the temperature could change so suddenly, it was supposed to be a nice night."

Grabbing her bathrobe Zenny said, "Do you remember when I told you that things like this were going to happen?" Zenny continued on without waiting for an answer. Well, I want you to know it's going to get even worse. The temperature fluctuation during the day or the night will become extreme, so much so, that you won't really know how to dress for the weather. I know that at some point the temperature differences between the cold and hot will be over eighty degrees or more at any given time."

Looking into her friends eyes, Zenny realized that she may have said too much. In a softer voice, as the wind quieted, Zenny said, "I'm sorry, I didn't mean to upset you."

Jessica turned to her friend and replied, "I've given thought to my answer ... yes, I want to know."

The two briefly embraced and then walked into the kitchen to make some tea to help take the chill out of their bones as Zenny told Jessica of the coming events.

Sleep for Jessica that night didn't come easily, for thoughts of the future burned like embers in her mind. She was grateful that Zenny told her what was to come, for now she was able to better understand all the strange events that were going on around her. She usual began to understand why people seemed to have changed so dramatically and quickly over the past couple of years.

Chapter Eight

Many more days had passed as Zenny waited to hear from or see any sign of her mysterious dream person. As she waited, she tried to put into play all that was told to her. She did her best to treat people fairly and kindly. She tried to tell people about the things she had been told in her dreams, but most turned a deaf ear, or looked at her as if she had come from some other planet, and they would dismiss her as being psychotic.

Feeling dejected, Zenny went about her life and waited for more information.

Several nights later....

"Have you been paying attention my dear? Are you looking to the skies? Have you noticed the suns and other planets coming closer to the Earth?

There are now three suns in the sky, one is yellow, one is red, the other is blue. I understand that the yellow sun no longer looks yellow, it appears white. This is because of the other suns which are causing the yellow sun to glow 'white hot', this is not a good thing, for our Earth will be burned to a crisp if the other two suns continue to progress forward towards the Earth.

Have you taken note of the incoming planets? One is red, this planet can cause the Earth to go into a freezing period. The other planet, which is green, is also, coming towards the Earth and that planet will cause more earthquakes, landslides, and volcanoes.

What does this mean for the world as a whole? It means that parts of the world could be thrown into an instant ice-age, while other parts of the world could have spontaneous beams of heat that burst forth from the reflection of the planets; until the land is turned into molten glass.

What about the other parts of the world, well perhaps those will end up with scalding days and freezing nights, rather like a desert. But, this will be even more extreme, with the chance of a 245* temperature change within a twenty-four hour period.

Is it possible for people of the world to exist with such extremes of climate? Yes and no. It will depend on how well they are prepared by our people. We are here to guide the people and to help them survive the coming events, if the Earth does not change it ways.

Zenny interjected into her dream and asked, "Are these things that will be or may be?"

Oh, I see you are paying attention; that is good. These are things that will most likely be, however, the Earth's vibrations are very fluid and we change with them. But, no matter what takes place we are here to help the people adjust to their new ways of life. If the aforementioned version comes to pass, then we will teach the people how to live underground or above, depending upon their location. It is survivable, but the people must be prepared. For if the time comes, they must act quickly and not hesitate.

The people on Earth must wakeup, *and understand that the things they have been told are all a lie. Most of history has been falsified to suit* the winner. Even the most recent past events have changed because of the easy manipulation of data on a computer. That is why the majority of people don't really know how to write a sentence or even speak a sentence correctly, for they have been using the machines for too many years. Their intelligence has dropped by many points.

Zenny interjected again, "are you saying that I am stupid and not using the full potential of my of brain power?"

You are not stupid, however, you also aren't using your full potential, for you haven't been taught how to do so. Now allow me to continue, for I must be leaving you soon. As I was saying, it will be up to Time to decide who will leave the Earth before the events come to pass. Those who are not allowed to leave are to stay and repent for their fallen ways. If they do not repent, then their fates will be sealed on Earth, for they will not be allowed to enter into the heavens. Also, some may choose to stay on Earth to help others. Some may choose to stay on Earth for their loved ones still remain. It will be mostly up to the individual as to their fate.

The time for us to meet has come. I will see you by the end of this week. Good-night my sweet child, and sleep well.

Chapter Nine

Waking refreshed and feeling delighted in the knowledge of knowing that she was finally going to meet the person who has been haunting her dreams, Zenny felt exhilarated as she and Jessica hopped onto the Levotrain. During their brief ride to work, Zenny continued to tell Jessica what she could about the dreams and the possible events that are yet to come. The only detail she left out, was that she would be meeting the person from her dream some time this week.

The work week dragged on for Zenny as she waited impatiently for the mysterious person from her dream. By the time Friday came, she began doubting what she had heard in her dream. Riding the Levotrain home with Jessica, the two talked about Keen and how Jessica and he were back together.

Zenny said, "I hope this time you two will be able to work out your differences and that things will be better for the both of you."

"I think things will be well this time," Jessica replied back. He promised me that he would never ...." the Levotrain doors opened. Stepping out into the extremely bright sunlight Jessica was about to finish her sentence when she noticed a very tall, masculine dark-haired man standing next to the train.

"Hello ladies," he called out.

Blushing, Jessica replied, "Hi."

Zenny lowered her head for she knew her eyes would give away the intense feelings that were coursing through her body. A flush swam through her small frame as she replied softly, "Hi."

"Are you two coming from WebNet?" the man questioned.

Eagerly Jessica answered, "Yes. We work the day shift." Wanting to continue to converse with this handsome looking man, Jessica continued, "Where do you work?"

"I have my own business," he replied.

"Self-employed, that's a rare thing these days," she replied as she nudged Zenny into trying to get her to talk with the man. Although Jessica found him attractive, she knew that Zenny would be a better match, besides she had to remember that she and Keen were trying to get back together.

The nudge only made matters worse for Zenny, for she was having trouble controlling the quivers which were beginning to take over her body.

"You're a quiet one, aren't you?" the man questioned directly to Zenny.

Coming out in almost a squeak, Zenny answered, "Not usually. I think it's just the brightness of the day." A sudden rambling of words spewed out her mouth as she said, "I'm hot, I'm thirsty, and I really just want to get something to eat." Looking down at her high-heeled feet in embarrassment for her sudden outburst of words, Zenny said nothing more.

"Perhaps I can talk you ladies into getting some refreshments with me and possibly some dinner, since you're hungry," he said quirking a smile as he looked directly as Zenny, who continued her lowered gaze.

"Oh that would be wonderful," Jessica piped in.

Turning towards her friend, Zenny said, "I really think we should be getting home."

"What's the rush?" the man piped in. "Do you have a date tonight? I promise I won't keep you long. Perhaps we might turn out to be friends," he said warmly.

Zenny wanted to get home in hopes that the dream person would eventually show up, but reluctantly she agreed after Jessica jabbed her in the ribs once again with her elbow. She knew her friend was just trying to be helpful. Jessica knew that Zenny's break-up with Collin, which had happened several months ago, had been so hard on her.

Reluctantly Zenny replied, "Alright, but only for one beverage."

The strange man and Jessica both nodded in agreement.

Chapter Ten

The trio went over to the corner depot and entered in. Taking a seat at the small round table near a corner, the three sat down.

"I suppose we should get the introductions out of the way," the man smiled warmly. "My name is Turris, and you two are?"

"I'm Jessica."

"I'm Zen'obia, but you can call me Zenny."

That's quite an interesting name, Turris said as he nodded his assent when the women spoke their names. "Did you know the spoken word has much power?" he questioned the two women.

Jessica shook her head no and Zenny nodded yes.

Trying to make Zenny feel more comfortable, Turris asked, "How do you two know each other, is it from work?"

Jumping in with the answer, Jessica replied, "From work and we also share a small house together." For some reason this man didn't really worry her, for Jessica that was unusual, for she was a naturally suspicious woman.

Turning towards Zenny he said, "I suppose we should order something to drink and then maybe you will be more open to talking," he said quirking a half smile.

The waitress came to the table and asked what they wanted to drink. All three ordered an orange juice with ice in it. They smiled at each other as they placed the order.

Moments later the waitress came back with their drinks.

Shortly after receiving their drinks, Jessica dismissed herself to use the restroom without asking Zenny if she wanted to come with. Jessica wanted her friend and Turris to get to know each other. She thought they would make an interesting couple.

As Jessica exited the table, Turris said in hushed tones, "I'm glad she left, it will give me a moment to talk with you alone."

Zenny eyes opened wide not understanding his motives.

Chapter Eleven

"Do you not recognize me?" Turris questioned.

"Should I?" Zenny replied with suspicion in her voice.

"You have been waiting for someone, have you not?" he questioned.

A blush ran over her face, but uncertain of his intent, she kept silent.

"Do you not hear me in your dreams? Did I not say that we would meet by the end of this week?" Turris prodded.

Still not taking the bait, for Zenny waited for more information.

Knowing he needed to prove himself, he said, "I have come to you in your dreams. I have spoke to you about the things to come. I have told you that the events in the world my be very tragic. Do you remember me now?"

Nodding her head in agreement, Zenny said, I thought you would be a woman … well I mean that I never really knew what you were, you were just a nondescript voice that came to me in the night."

"That's understandable," he replied, "and that is done on purpose. We don't want to put any undue thoughts into a person's head. We need for them to focus on what we are saying and why we are saying it. Do you understand?"

"Yes, I suppose it makes sense," Zenny admitted.

Jessica came walking back to the table and said, "Well, I'm going to be on my way." Zenny are you ready to leave or are you going to stay longer?"

"I think I'll stay a bit longer," Zenny responded to her friend. "I will call you before I leave so you know when to expect me home, okay?" Zenny told Jessica knowing that she would worry about her safety.

Bending over and hugging her friend's shoulder, Jessica whispered into her ear, "Do you feel safe with him? Would you like me to stay?" Then she added, "He's really cute."

Whispering back, Zenny replied, "I will be perfectly safe with him, for he is the one who has been in my dreams."

Feeling a sense of relief, knowing that her fried would be fine, Jessica smiled kindly and waved good-night then left for home.

Chapter Twelve

After Jessica left the depot, Turris slid his chair next to Zenny so their conversation would not be as easily heard by others.

With not much time, Turris said, "We need to begin things quickly. I wish I would have been allowed to come to you *much* sooner, but Time did not allow it."

"Why did you choose me to talk with at night?" Zenny questioned.

"Time gives us multiple people to speak with at night and those who choose to hear are the ones that are of value, but those who dismiss the words as just dreams are left behind."

"How many people do you talk with at night?"

"I began with fifty, but am now down to five."

"So, it's myself and four others that know this information?" Zenny queried.

"Sort of, the other forty-five have some of the knowledge, but not fully." His voice turning serious he added, "They can be dangerous under certain conditions. All we can do is hope that they don't use the information against us when the time comes."

Leaning in closer so their elbows almost touched, Zenny questioned, "What is it that you need me to do and when and how do I do it?" she inquired with hesitation in her voice.

"You don't need to fear," he replied, trying to calm her worries. "Time only gives us what each of us can handle."

"Do you take all your directions from Time or is some of it up to the individual?"

"Not all the directions are from Time, and yes some of it, is up to each of us. We take what Time tells us and we then put it into human terms and actions. Then we do the best that we can. And that is all that Time asks of us. He knows we are human and we make human mistakes, He just doesn't want us to go completely off on our own, He wants to guide us to do the right things."

"Wow! That feels like quite a burden," she replied honestly.

"Don't worry, if you choose to join us, we will help you along the way. There are many of us, but no where near enough to heal the world from all its corruption."

"When do I get to meet the others?"

"You will be meeting them this weekend if you accept this responsibility," he said as he leaned in closer to Zenny.

"Well, that is soon. How do you know I don't have plans already," she teased.

Easing back a bit with a smile, he said, "If you did I would have to ask you to cancel them." Looking around the room, Turris continued, "I think it would be wise of us to stop for the night. Too many people are coming in for supper." Then as an after thought, he added, "Would you like to have something to eat?"

Nodding her head gratefully, she said, "Yes."

The night continued on as the two became acquainted with each other. Turris didn't bring up the matter of help for the rest of the night. When the two finished their meals, Turris said, "May I walk you home?"

"I would like that," Zenny replied and continued, "I had a nice time."

"I think it's important that we get to know each other since we will be spending a lot of time together," he replied honestly, then added, "I will come to your house in the morning and pick you up so we can get started."

"Sounds good to me. What time?" she questioned.

"Eight a.m."

Nodding her agreement, the two left the depot and Turris walked her the few blocks home.

Chapter Thirteen

Standing at the entrance to Zenny's house, Turris said, "I'm glad we were finally able to meet."

"Me too," Zenny replied.

Hesitating Turris said, "When we speak with people in their sleep, we only know if they are a male or a female, but we are not allowed to see what they look like ... I must say ... I'm was pleasantly surprised to see that you are ... I mean, I'm glad to know I will be your guide," a light blush crossed over his masculine face. For the whole night he had kept the mood light and tried not to focus on his growing thoughts for this woman. But, for the moment, he wanted to know if she was beginning to feel the same way.

Seeing the nervous shuffle of his feet and the anxious movements of his body, gave Zenny a warm feeling. But, she wasn't quite certain why he reacted this way.

"I'm also happy that you will be my guide," she smiled warmly.

Opening the door to her house, Zenny walked in and bid Turris a good-night.

Seeing the door open, from her seat on the couch, Jessica began to bombard Zenny with questions, "Do you like him? He's attractive, isn't he. When are you going to meet again?"

"Jessica, I just walked in the door," Zenny said with a teasing smile, the added, "He can probably hear you through the door. Let's just give it a few minutes. Besides, I need to use the bathroom," she added with a giggle as she proceed to leave the room and head for the restroom.

Patiently, Jessica waited for Zenny to return to the room and tell her all about the night. A few minutes later, Zenny entered the room. The two women began to talk. Their conversation went on for over two hours. Zenny finally said, "Well, it's been a long night. I told you all I can for now. I must get ready for bed. As I told you, I have to meet Turris tomorrow morning."

"Oh yes, I won't keep you any longer. Good-night Zenny," Jessica said as she watched Zenny stand up.

"Good-night Jessica," Zenny replied.

Chapter Fourteen

Morning came sooner than Zenny had anticipated. Jumping out of bed at 7:30 a.m., she rushed to eat breakfast, then hurried to ready herself.

A gentle knock on the door made Zenny jump. Since it was the weekend, Jessica decided to sleep-in, so Zenny went to the door and answered it.

"Good-morning," Turris said. "Are you prepared for the day?"

"Oh yes!" she replied excitedly. "I'm anxious to learn all that is needed to help you and your kind with the events in the world."

"That's a good attitude to have. There really is a lot of work to be done," Turris replied kindheartedly as he continued, "We will take my mode of transportation, if that's alright with you?"

"Yes, it's fine." Looking out the open door, she questioned, "Where is it?"

"There," he pointed to the air flyer.

"Oh my!" she exclaimed. I've only seen those in showroom windows, but I've never seen one in person. I thought they were smaller."

"Some are," he replied, but this a two seater. We only have three of them, for they're rather costly, but we use the ones with the two seats when we go to pick up new recruits."

"I think it is very impressive," Zenny replied, then added, "I'm glad they are making them in white now, especially since the sun is so strong most of the time."

"Yes, we did have the option of a different color, but this is the one that makes the most sense for the times we are living in."

The two hopped into the the air flyer and Zenny said as they began to take off, "What makes this type of craft fly, since there aren't any wings? Do you know what keeps them aloft?

"It's a gravitational wave. It's used for lift off, flight, and landing."

"That is so interesting," Zenny replied excitedly, as she looked out the large window in front of her.

Zenny looked at how the window wrapped around the upper part of the doors and over the upper part of the front of the flyer. The back of the craft was made of a solid, flexible type of steel. The exact method of making the steel was highly classified. It was a great material to work with, for once it was in place it kept its shape. The material could also be remelted and reshaped easily, after it had cooled, then it had the flexibility and ease of use, rather like tinfoil.

As they flew, Zenny watched the ground as it grew smaller. She felt her cares and burdens lessen, as they removed themselves from the hold of the Earth. Taking a deep breath and letting out a deep sigh, Zenny leaned back and watched the world go by. But, all too soon, they were landing at an unspecified location, one which Zenny had never seen before.

Chapter Fifteen

Departing the small craft, Zenny stepped out and was taken aback by the strong heat, from the, white-hot sun. It felt as if it were burning her skin.

"My it's hot," Zenny said to Turris. "I didn't expect it to be so blazing outside today."

"Did you bring an umbrella or screen with you?" Turris questioned.

"No, I didn't. I guess that's why I usually plan ahead, but this time I was so exited, I didn't think about it," Zenny replied.

Looking towards the sandy, barren expanse that splayed out before the her, Zenny asked Turris, "Where are we to go? I don't see anything but sand."

"It's just up ahead. You can't see it from here and that's the way it has to be," he replied as he added, "It's for our safety."

"Is it a long walk?" Zenny questioned as they began their steps forward.

"No, not too long, it's about 550 yards ahead. We should start seeing the sun canopy," Turris replied. "We'll be inside before the intensity of the sun effects us," he said reassuringly.

As they walked, Zenny commented in amazement, "Why didn't I see the canopy from the air?"

"It's made that way to keep the Mooncalves from finding where we congregate."

"Why do they pursue your kind?"

"They find us to be a threat," then he added, "You keep saying, 'your kind', but you must remember, you are just the same as we are. "It's just that you haven't had the teachings that we've had," he said a bit too gruffly. Feeling annoyed that Zenny seemed to be implying that 'they' were some kind of freaks.

Looking away from his hurt gaze, Zenny continued her steps, not saying anything more, until Turris spoke.

As they neared the entrance Turris said, "If you are chosen, and then, if you choose to join us, you too may be pursued. But, that is something that only time will tell."

Walking down numerous steps to the door, Turris said, "Are you ready?"

Zenny nodded.

Chapter Sixteen

Upon entering the enclosure, Turris called out to a man standing in the corner of the large subterranean room, "Otto!"

Otto turned to Turris and replied, "Hey! It's good to see you. This must be the new recruit?"

"Yes, her name is Zenny."

"Nice to meet you, Zenny," Otto said with genuine enthusiasm.

"Nice to meet you, Otto," Zenny replied warmly.

"Are you ready to discover things that you never thought possible?" Otto inquired.

"Mmm, I guess so," Zenny said with a blush crossing over her face. She didn't know what caused this sudden flush, but chalked it up to the excitement of being someplace new.

Zenny continued, "I hope that I can live up to what is expected of me."

"We don't really expect anything of the new recruits, we just want to find out if you're really on our side, or the side of the Mooncalves. Then when it's time, you will have to be approved by the elders."

"I didn't know that I needed approval. I thought I was chosen to do this," Zenny remarked to Otto feeling confused.

"Well yes and no," Otto answered. Turning towards Turris he said, "Didn't you tell her about the elders?"

Embarrassment washed over Turris' body as he shifted uncomfortably and replied, "She's a natural. I'm certain she'll be accepted."

Looking questioningly at Turris, Otto said nothing more to the man and turned is attention to Zenny. "Well, you will have to go through a few tests. But, if Turris is confident in your approval, then you really don't have to worry too much about it. But, for now, we can show you around."

Realizing that Turris had inadvertently missed telling her about the elders, she questioned Otto, "Isn't it dangerous for you to show me how to get to this place? What if I'm not approved?"

"As I said before, there is no need to worry about the approval. And no, it's not really dangerous for us, because no one would be able to find this place unless they had the proper directions, or if they knew how to get here by heart. There aren't any defining landmarks, and with the consistent shifting of the sand, there aren't any trails to follow. So we don't worry about it." Then he added with a well defined smile on his square face, "We also have a cloaking canvas, which was given to us by the Svadilfari to help us; to help hide our location."

"Ooh, that's really interesting!" Zenny said with excitement. "Who are the Svadilfaris'?"

Taking Zenny by the hand, Otto lead her to a photo on the wall. "These are the Svadilfaris.'"

Quizzically, she said, "They look like a tribe from many eons ago. I thought this type of village no longer existed."

"Sadly, as of five years ago, they all died out, except for Svadilfari himself," Otto said with a hint of sadness in his voice. "The Svadifari's had named him such, for they wanted to be remembered. They knew he was the last of their kind. Since then, Svadilfari has lived with us." Shaking his head, Otto continued, "It's hard to believe that with all their technology, they still were unable to keep the village going. They just didn't have enough of their kind left, and they wouldn't allow any other type of person to mix with them."

Shaking her head, not fully understanding, Zenny heard Turris say, "It's time we moved on."

Turris didn't like the closeness that seemed to begin to form between Zenny and Otto. He couldn't place the feeling, but he knew he didn't like it.

Smiling a toothy smile, Otto said, "We'll talk again."

With a bit too much of force, Turris took Zenny by the arm and lead her away.

Zenny turned her head towards Otto as she felt herself being pulled away and nodded her response with a smile to Otto.

Chapter Seventeen

An hour later, Turris had shown Zenny all the alcoves and various rooms which were abound in this subterranean hideout. Some of the rooms held labs, while others were sleeping quarters.

As they walked down a long, narrow hallway, Turris said, "When you and the other recruits become members, you will be given a room for sleeping."

"What makes you so sure that I'll be allowed to stay?" Zenny asked Turris, sensing a coolness coming from his attitude towards her.

"I just have a feeling that there won't be a problem," he replied trying to hid his feelings from the intuitive woman. He too, was getting the sense that she could feel the aloofness, which he had been showing her, ever since they left Otto.

With his next words, he tried to talk more gently, as he said, "We have one central kitchen. It is shared by all the people who work and live here. They can cook any time they want to. We also have the option to wait until the meals are prepared by the cooks in the kitchen. It's really up to each person, also it has to do with when their schedule will allow," Turris said.

"So, if someone works late at night and the cooks aren't working, they can go and make some food for themselves?" Zenny said more as a statement then an actual question.

Turris, nodded his reply.

Chapter Eighteen

After the tour, Zenny wondered out loud as they stood in a large, open hall, "Why don't all of you, just live the rest of your lives down here where it is safe and away from the Mooncalves?"

"If that is what Time would instruct us to do, then we would do it, but that is not what *He* is requesting of us," Turris replied.

"Has the thought ever crossed anyone's mind to just hide out here?" Zenny questioned peering her soft face up towards the tall man standing before her.

"If it has," Turris said honestly, "no one has voiced it to me."

Looking around at the medium sized village inside the subterranean hideout, Zenny continued, "I certainly wouldn't mind living down here for the rest of my life. It has everything and none of the violence and corruption from above."

Worrisome thoughts emanated through his voice, as Turris said, "That's not what we are here for." Turris suddenly felt that Zenny might not be strong enough to handle what may be asked of her. He could tell the Zenny felt uncomfortable with his sudden statement.

Realizing that she caused Turris concern over her sincerity, Zenny said, trying to ease the tense situation, "I didn't mean to say, that, that is something I would do, I just meant, that I feel at home here, and if the need should ever arise and Time would allow it, then I wouldn't mind staying here."

Seeing her blushing face, Turris replied, with a deep inhalation, "Well that's enough for now. How about we get something to eat? I think they should be serving lunch about now."

"That's sounds good to me, I'm hungry."

Placing his hand upon the small of Zenny's back, he ushered her out of the large hall.

Moments later they were walking into the dining area. Numerous people were milling about talking and eating. Zenny didn't pay much attention to what the people were saying, for it all seemed to become a mumbled mass of words as they neared the large group of people.

———•———

AFTER THEY HAD FINISHED their meal, Zenny had one more question before they left the area. "Turris?"

"Mmm?" he responded as he wiped his face with a cloth napkin.

"I noticed a lot of people are here, and they seem to be in pairs, is this normal?"

"For now it is. The pairs of people you see, are recruits just like you. After we have the supper meal, in a few hours from now, that is when each of the potential candidates find out if they are a good fit for us. And as you know, if they aren't they will be brought back to their homes to continue on with their lives. If they are a good fit, then they will be sent the the elders for their final approval. Sometimes that can take days, other times, weeks.

"Oh, that's a long time," Zenny said with a concerned look. Then she added, "Shouldn't things be done sooner, since all of this is very important?"

"Don't worry. If Time wanted us to do things more quickly, we would know about it, " he said with a smile, as his body finally began to ease. Yet, he still had feelings for this woman that confounded him and they just kept gnawing at his insides. For the briefest of moments a feeling of deep love coursed through his veins, but he shook it off. He didn't know much about this woman, so he didn't want to think about such things, for now was not the time for such endeavors.

Chapter Nineteen

By the time supper arrived, Zenny had found out a great deal about this underground village. She even found out a little bit more about herself. She learned that her name told of a woman who had great courage, was high spirited and had extraordinary beauty. She also learned what some of the other people's names meant, such as Turris. His name seemed to have different meanings, it would just depend on which country would it was used in. Some say it was a high, rocky hill, other countries would say it was a rock or crag. Some said it was a lofty hill or mound. But, the most popular seemed to be a 'high structure'. As for Turris, himself, he just would say that it meant something of a high place. For Svadilfari, the man who created the cloaking device, his name came from a stallion that had magical powers. She found their names intriguing.

Some of the things that Zenny learned, were hard for her to accept, but she knew in time, she would understand them fully. She found out that the world has been thrown off kilter, and is now tipped and wobbling every day. Even the time has changed.

When Turris told Zenny of the time issue, she replied, "How can that be? People would notice such a thing."

Turris replied to her query, "Over the next few months, while you're being taught on our ways, get a digital time piece and a battery powered or wind up clock. Set both clocks to the exact time. Then after a few months, check to see if the digital clock shows a faster time. You will notice that it is faster by three or more minutes. This is not a malfunction of the non-digital clock, but a result of the Earth's rotation being thrown off kilter."

Zenny agreed and said that she would go to a shop the next day and try to find a non-digital clock and try the experiment for herself. She thought that people would notice such a time difference, but soon, she would find out that all of what Turris said was true.

Turris had told her that the world does not live in a single solar system, but it is actually a trinary system. He told her that there are two other objects which are orbiting very close to the sun. Time had not told him if they were other planets, suns, or possibly some other foreign objects. But, this made no difference, for it was viewable if a person paid attention to the sky. Zenny also learned how the objects came around once every three thousand-six hundred years. These objects cause the sun to look white when all three are within close proximity of each other. The objects come closer together after sunrise and an hour or so before sunset, thus causing the sun to look white. When they are a bit further apart in their orbit, the morning sun will take on an orange, pink, or purple hue, just as the setting sun will also do. It depends on which of the objects is closest to the sun. One of the objects is blue in color and the other is red in color. These objects also cause, the moon to do things that it normally wouldn't do. With increasing closeness to the proximity of the Earth, it begins to cause havoc worldwide. This event has been known to humans since they were first placed upon the Earth, but has been kept from them by the Mooncalves. The Mooncalves believe that people are too stupid and too quick to react to such things.

As the objects hurdle near the Earth, various events could happen. It may cause: increased Tornado's with higher EF numbers; more volcanoes; larger floods; strange weather events in unusual places; and many other things that could create the downfall of humanity. People would become morally deprived, idol worship could becomes a predominate place in culture. Children and many adults could be drawn into the worshiping of movie stars, singers, dancers, ecetera. Many people would turn towards their idols for their opinions, beliefs, and to know how to act in their daily lives, rather than using common sense and turning their faith and love to the source of all ... *Time*.

The Mooncaves have known about these events for many generations, something which they keep secreted to themselves. They promote the idol worship, so they are then able to create more moral depravity and allow the rotting of souls to feed the idol which they worship. They hope that by feeding *their beast*, that it will then save them from annihilation.

Time is the only one who has control over life and death. *He* tries to waken the people from their slumber and pull them away from material things. *He* wants His people to prosper, but *He* also wants their acceptance and to listen to his teachings. *He* has always told His people to be prepared and keep themselves able to provide for all their necessities through their own abilities. *He* had taught them, when to begin to prepare, what would happen, and how to prepare for it. It was all written for the people to see. But *His* words have blown away, like dust blows away in the wind.

Chapter Twenty

After supper Turris said, "Here is a booklet that is specifically for you." Handing the booklet to Zenny he continued, "Be certain to read it by Tuesday. I will stop by your house and we will talk more then."

Accepting the booklet, Zenny said, "Are these my tests?"

Turris nodded.

After leaving the dining hall, the two boarded the air flyer. Zenny leaned back in the seat and closed her eyes. Her mind was reeling. Thoughts coursed through her brain as millions of neurons fired simultaneously. She couldn't keep a coherent thought, so she said nothing.

Finally reaching her home, Zenny let out a sigh as Turris said, "Try to get some sleep. I know today has been overwhelming for you."

Zenny smiled and walked into the quiet house. Jessica was not at home, for she was out with Keen.

Strolling over to her bedroom, Zenny looked at the heading of the booklet, it read:

Creation, Creatures, Cremation

Under the title was written:

First: Create divine ones.

Second: Make miraculous signs in the heavens.

Third: Create land.

Fourth: Make abundant flora and fauna, food and herbs of all kinds.

Fifth: Create beasts and beings.

Feeling a bit of panic, Zenny thought that those where the things she had to do for her test. But, she continued to read on wondering what it all meant.

Entry One: We were told by our fore-fathers to follow the inviolable words which were given to them by Time. Many have tried over the eons, most have failed. We the Second Reborns, shall try again! We were born unto Emily, Jacob, and Asher. They brought us into being. We must not fail them again.

Entry Two: The whole land was soft with mud. Its viscosity was inconsistent. Parts of the land were like taffy, some were bogs, other parts were completely covered in a purple fluid which spewed from the belly of the Earth.

The waters had turned from clear to murky, taking on a putrid odor and had the appearance of urine. After all these generations, we are now seeing some of the land become solid again, but not in the way which one would have been familiar with.

The hardened land is consistent with that of wood. There is much confusion and many things feel unreal. We have, as yet, to figure out how to make this land viable. We currently live in the mire where we must wear our metallic suits to allow us to walk upon the boggy surface and proceed downwards into our homes, lest we are swallowed up by the viscous brown taffy-like substance.

Entry Three: The Mooncalves are a consistent threat to our survival. They seem to need to make us capitulate to their ways, but we know we must not give in. Their ways are strong and we are few. Every time we start to terraform the land, they find it and use their highly advanced weapons upon it to destroy whatever amount of solidity there is.

Entry Four: Emptiness is all around. We venture out only during the full moon, for we know that mother Emily will protect us. The brave have tried many times during the day to help reshape the Earth, but it is all in vain. The Mooncalves find them and destroy them.

Entry Five: In the beginning the Mooncalves captured many of the First Reborns. They wanted to try to find out why they were so special. They wanted to harness their powers and abilities, but to no avail. So they began systematically to exterminate all that lived.

Entry Six: We, the Second Generation are more prepared and cautious, even when there is a full moon, for mother Emily is unable to protect all. She once spoke to our ancestors, the First Reborns, about her mother, Mother Earth. Earth is on hiatus as per Time's instructions. We are to learn from our past and stop trying to hide from it. It is up to us to renew the Earth and all that what once was.

Entry Seven: We have noticed strange and different species. These things are not to be on this Earth. We feel the Mooncalves are creating them to fright against us. We must continue to try. If we fail in this generation, then the following generation will be burdened with having to continue to fight our war. We must prevail. I don't know if this is what Time wants, but we will continue our endeavors and carry on with our tasks.

Entry Eight: They are here! They have found our subterranean village! I speculate that one of our own turned astray and betrayed us. I know not what is to take place next. I know that I will fight until I die. I will not surrender, I will fight for peace, for I will NOT live in tyranny!

Entry Nine: This may be my last entry. They are now within one-half mile from where I reside.

I am given a memory, a quote that mother Emily had written; I believe it went something like this:

> *"Give not that which is holy unto the dogs,*
> *neither cast ye your pearls before swine,*
> *lest they trample them under their feet,*

and turn again and rend you."

Somehow this quote seems fitting now. I will not give them my gift. I will not give them my soul. I hear them coming! The thunderous sound of their feet upon the ground is unmistakable. Though my legs aren't as strong as they once were, I will stand before them and await my judgment.

There were no further entries. Zenny set the booklet down, placed her face into her palms, and wept. She knew she was reading the dairy of someone long forgotten. She knew that this war was not a new one. She knew the re-forming of the Earth had transpired many times before. And to read the final moments before the persons death was unbearable. This was all too much for her. She dropped back onto her bed and fell into a deep, fitful sleep. Dreams plagued her as images washed over her mind. Wanting to wake from the night terrors which gripped her body, Zenny thrashed about on her bed until the intense morning sun finally woke her from her slumber.

Chapter Twenty-One

Tuesday came all too soon. Zenny wasn't certain if she could bear the trials that were to come, not only from the elders, but also that she may have to protect the Earth from the Mooncalves, when the time comes. The burden weighed heavily on her mind. How could *she* wake people from their slumber, how could she make people stop believing what the Mooncalves were preaching? They control the media, papers, WebNet, and all forms of communications. How could *she* be of any help.

"Knock, knock."

Startling Zenny back from her thoughts, she walked over to the door and ushered Turris into her home.

Seeing her beseeching look, Turris said, "I see you read the booklet." Pausing for a moment to collect his thoughts he added, "It *is* difficult for many to read the words of our ancestors. Unfortunately it is all true." Placing a reassuring hand upon her small shoulder, he continued, "Every new generation is in charge of keeping our books safe, otherwise the Mooncalves get a hold of them and put them into a museum for storage, where they are never seen again." Wrapping his arm about her waist, he walked Zenny over to the couch where they both sat down. He asked her, "Do you have any questions for me?"

Shaking her head softly, she replied, "No. I feel at a loss for words. I feel drained."

"These feelings are normal," Turris replied. Give yourself some time, but also know, that I am here for you." Softly lifting her hand from Zenny's side, Turris asked gently, "Are you ready for today?"

Looking into his deep brown eyes, Zenny replied, "I know this is what must be done. I know that I was chosen for this task." Looking down at his hand, as it grasped hers, she replied, "As long as you are there to guide me, and keep me focused, I feel that I will be okay." Looking at his softly parted lips she added, "I feel comfortable with you."

Seeing deep emotions in Zenny's bright green eyes, the brazen man leaned in and gently kissed her softly on the lips.

A weight seemed to lift off of her burden laden shoulders. All too soon, the brief kiss ended. Breathing in deeply, she said, "Thank you."

Turris, wasn't certain how his kiss would be accepted, but he was glad to find that she found it reassuring and pleasant. He also felt his feelings growing very quickly for this intriguing woman. She had such gentleness, kindness, and an aura about her, that Turris found it hard to turn his gaze away.

After a few minutes of talking, the two left for the subterranean village.

Chapter Twenty-Two

Otto saw Zenny and Turris enter the building. Walking to greet the two, Otto called out with outstretched arms, pulling her into a warm, friendly embrace saying, "Welcome back Zenny."

Otto was curious as to how Turris would react, for he wanted to rile his friend up just a bit. Otto knew that Turris has feelings for Zenny, but didn't want to admit the feelings to himself.

With a crooked smile upon his lips, Otto said to Turris, as he continued his light embrace around Zenny's waist, "I see our girl has decided to come back. That's a good sign."

Turris grunted his response.

Otto smiled to himself, now knowing that Turris was jealous.

Grasping Zenny's hand, Turris pulled Zenny away from Otto. Giving Otto a stern look, he said to Zenny, "We will go into this room."

Otto snickered as the two walked away.

"Here are some of the writing implements and paper. You are to document all that you are told to do and give your interpretations, as to how you feel about the situation. For today, you will be given an objective. It is sitting on the table. After I exit the room, read the objective and do as you see fit. Do you understand?"

"Yes," Zenny replied.

Taking a seat at the table Turris handed the items to Zenny and left the room.

OPENING THE PAPER ON the table, it read:

Go into the void where the secret places are. Above the corner in the abyss of darkness you will see space. You will need to speak with the divine ones. They will hover over you and judge your integrity for truth. If you are approved you will be able to continue onto step two.

Seeing a door in the far corner Zenny walked cautiously over to it and opened it. Peering inside she saw a light.

A voice called out to her, "Do as was written on the paper."

Walking into the secret place, she followed the deep void which held no light except directly in front of her. As she approached a corner in the darkness she saw a void, which appear to lead somewhere and yet nowhere. It was murky with a purple haze covering the area.

"Step into the area," the voice said.

Zenny did as she were told. She didn't fear the voice, but she did wonder about this strange place.

"Come forward Zenny," spoke the unseen voice once again.

Hesitantly stepping forwards Zenny moved her legs towards the voice.

"Do you fear us," questioned the voice?

"I don't know if I fear you, but I am concerned that I will not be allowed to help," she replied with a quiver in her throat.

Silence filled the air, then an utterance came in a commanding tone from a divine one. "Take this and use it to help you find your way."

Looking out before her, Zenny saw an item sitting on a small wooden table, it looked like a a small round orb filled with an opalescence of color. There were no buttons to push on the palm-sized orb, nor was there any hidden way to open it. The smooth glass ball which she was holding within her hands was warm to the touch, yet Zenny felt a calmness radiating from the orb flowing through her body. Uncertain as to how to use it she questioned, "Divine One, how am I to use this instrument? It is foreign to me."

"Do not question the orb," the divine one replied. "Look into your being and gaze into the orb to receive the answers that are necessary. If you are true, you will have the knowledge to use the object. If you are untrue, you shall be brought to task."

Unsteadily, Zenny glided one hand over the glowing object while cupping it underneath in her other hand. Feeling warmth fill her hand and spreading up into her arms, neck, shoulders, head, and then spilling over into her body, she felt a power grow within her.

"You are virtuous and wise," the divine one said. "You may now continue on."

Comprehending the depth of the item which she was given, Zenny replied, "Thank you for this gift."

Departing from the secret space, Zenny walked back to the room from which she came, holding the orb firmly within her hands.

Chapter Twenty-Three

Walking back to the table, Zenny saw another task written on a piece of paper, it read:

Place the orb inside the burlap sack and leave it on the table.
Find a friend.
If you feel the friend is worthy, bring the friend with you tomorrow.
If you are unable to find a worthy friend, come alone.

Moments later, the outer door opened. Zenny was glad to see Turris' handsome face.

"How did it go?" he questioned the wide-eyed woman standing beside the table. Looking down at the paper on the table he said, "I see you passed the first test. I'm glad for you." Continuing with his questions like a school boy, he said, "How do you feel about becoming a part of something that is much larger than yourself?" Continuing on without giving Zenny a chance to answer he said, "I remember when I was first accepted; I felt like I finally found where I belonged."

Zenny was smiling as she, watched Turris relive the time he was accepted. It made her heart feel lighter.

"It certainly helped boost my confidence knowing that we are 'light beings' and are gifted with extraordinary abilities," as Turris continued to relate his feelings to this woman that he had become very fond of. "I later learned that everyone has abilities with unlimited potential, but they are too absorbed in material things to practice their *Time* given gifts." Blushing in embarrassment as he realized that he was doing all the talking, Turris came close to Zenny, looking deeply into her green eyes saying, "Can you tell how happy I am for you?"

Leaning in to close the small gap, between Turris and herself, Zenny tipped-toed up and kissed his lips gently, showing her gratitude for having this intriguing man open her eyes to the real world.

An intense urge coursed through Turris' body, as he pulled the small woman in closer to his firm body. Feeling her small waist beneath his hands, Turris gently embraced her. The warmth of their bodies melded together into one, as their kiss deepened.

"Knock, knock," Otto called out at the closed door before him, "Can I enter?"

Grumbling under his breath, Turris moved his wanting body away from Zenny, as he replied, "You can enter."

"Did you pass the first task?" Otto questioned Zenny.

Zenny replied with a huge smile, "Yes!"

Chapter Twenty-Four

Soon Zenny was back at home, she wanted to talk to Jessica about having her come with her tomorrow. But, Jessica wasn't home. Impatiently she waited for her friend. A few hours later, Jessica entered the house after returning home from purchasing some food from the local gardener.

Zenny called out, "There you are." Looking at the bag of produce, Zenny said, "Was it costly?"

Jessica replied, "He gave me a discount so, it wasn't too expensive."

"That's good," Zenny said as she grabbed her bag and handed Jessica one-half of the amount that was written on the receipt.

"Thanks," Jessica replied.

"I have something to ask you," Zenny began hesitantly. Looking down at her feet she said, "Would you like to come with me tomorrow? I know you work, but this is important."

Jessica replied, "I know that you have used your vacation time this week, to go with Turris and see what he wants of you, but I don't know if I want to take a day off in the middle of the week. It seems rather pointless."

Becoming a little embarrassed, Zenny pressed on, "Well, as I said, it's rather important."

Seeing the concerned looked in her friend's eyes, Jessica responded, "Where would we be going?"

"I would like for you to come with me to the subterranean village. They would like to meet you," Zenny replied.

"Why me?" Jessica questioned.

"I was instructed to find a friend that I feel I can trust, and you are the one I thought of," Zenny replied. "I think you will find the place fascinating. I also, think you would learn some things that you didn't know or even consider thinking about."

"It's rather short notice for me to tell work," Jessica said feeling uncertain about what she might find out. *What if there were things there that she didn't want to know? What if she wanted to continue to live in this world and not in the world which Zenny appeared to want to inhabit?*

"Are you afraid?," Zenny questioned with concern in her voice, then added, "I will be there with you. I have met the people, they are very friendly and have treated me with kindness."

"Well, that's not what I'm worried about," Jessica replied.

"Then what could it be that is bothering you?" Zenny persisted.

"Do you really think it is something that I will enjoy?" Jessica asked.

"I don't know about enjoying it, but I do know you would learn a lot from it," Zenny answered.

Nodding her head, Jessica answered, "Okay. I'll let work know that I won't be coming in tomorrow and hopefully, I will learn something of importance. That way I won't feel as if I took off from work for nothing."

Smiling warmly, Zenny said sincerely, "Thank you. I really appreciate what you're doing for me."

With that, the two woman began to make their evening meal. During supper, Zenny told Jessica what to expect for the next day, but it seemed as if she wasn't really paying attention. That was okay with Zenny, for she really wanted to confide in her best friend, some of the things that she experienced while she was at the subterranean village. Zenny felt over-whelmed, yet eased by the things she had leaned today.

Chapter Twenty-Five

The next day came quickly for both women. Soon Turris was knocking upon their door. The three walked to the air flyer together. It wasn't long before they were at the subterranean village. As usual upon entering, Otto greeted Zenny and Turris. But, today he met the new possible recruit.

"Otto, I would like you to meet my friend Jessica," Zenny said to the stocky built man. "Jessica, this is Otto."

Otto and Jessica said both said, "Hello," at the same time. Then they both laughed. Otto felt an instant attraction towards Jessica and he sensed that the feeling was mutual.

Zenny noticed in Otto's eyes, his attraction towards her friend. She also noticed Jessica responding favorably to Otto. She had never thought that the two would make a couple, nor did it even cross her mind, especially since Jessica was dating Keen. But none-the-less, it was happening right before her eyes.

Turris had also noticed the instant attraction between the two. But his reaction was different. He felt relief that Otto found Jessica attractive, for then he would keep his eyes towards Jessica and not towards Zenny.

"Well ladies," Turris said, "We need to get the two of you to the room and see what is to happen next."

Jessica looked at Turris, as if, he had grown two heads as she questioned, "What do you mean, *to the room?*"

"Didn't you tell her?" Turris asked Zenny.

"I told her about it at supper," Zenny replied in her defense.

Turning towards Jessica, Turris asked in a mono-tone voice, "Is that true?"

With a light blush, Jessica nodded and said, "I wasn't really listening to what Zenny told me last night. I think I was more concerned about what work would think."

"Okay," Turris replied. Briefing Jessica on the events of the day, Turris said, "You and Zenny will be going to the room which Zenny did her first task. When you enter the room you will take a seat and wait for someone to come into the room. I think it will be Timothy, at that point you will be asked some questions regarding your beliefs towards the Mooncalves, and other various organizations. If the person asking the questions feels that you are a good fit for our subterranean village, then you will be accepted, *if* you choose to be a part of our society. If you choose not to stay, then you may leave and you won't be bothered again."

"Okay," was Jessica's brief response as they entered the room.

Chapter Twenty-Six

Timothy came into the room where the two women were. He looked at them and asked, "Are you ready to begin?"

Both nodded, yes.

Approximately an hour later, Timothy, the questioner left the room. The two women stayed in the room for another thirty minutes before Timothy came back and told them, that he had submitted his report and also, that both had been accepted. Moments later Jessica and Zenny left the room, smiling happily.

Jessica was accepted as part of the group to be a helper. She had until Saturday to decide if she would like to become part of the cause. But, Jessica didn't need until Saturday, for she had already made up her mind. She wanted to be a part of this place, for she found the purpose to be worth while and wanted to help in any way that she could. But also, there was the man who took her breath away the moment she met him. Jessica wanted to get to know him much better. No thoughts of Keen went through her mind, for now it was only filled with the thoughts of Otto.

As for Zenny, she too was accepted, but her placement wasn't set. She needed to be placed elsewhere. But, that wasn't up to Timothy to decide. He told Zenny that the elder's or someone with high authority would be the ones to place her.

AS THE TWO WOMEN EXITED the room they saw Turris approaching, and heard him call out, "I heard the both of you were accepted," he said with a wide grin on his face.

"News gets around fast," Zenny replied with a smile.

"Most of the time it does," Turris answered, "but, this time it's because I saw Timothy in the hallway and asked him if the two of you were accepted."

Looking at Jessica, Zenny said, "I'm so glad Jessica was accepted. She's my best friend."

"Thanks," Jessica said with a wide grin on her delighted face.

"Remember, you don't need to decide right away," Turris said, knowing that it is a big decision to make, "You can take a couple of days to decide."

"My mind's made up," Jessica replied with firm resolve, "I've decide to become a part of all of this. I think it is worth my time and I really want for people to wake up to what is really happening in the world, especially before it is too late."

"That's wonderful to hear," Turris responded. "Since you've decided to stay, I will have Otto show you around. I'm sure he should be coming along soon."

Seeing Otto in the distance, Turris called out to him, "Otto, would you come over here for a moment?"

Turning towards the approaching man, Jessica's eyes lit up as she saw Otto coming towards them.

"Otto," Turris said, "Would you show Jessica around? I have to take Zenny to the room for her placement. She was accepted, but she wasn't placed."

Nodding happily, Otto said to Jessica, "Right this way, my lady. Timothy told me you were accepted. I'm glad to have heard such good news," he said with a wide grin on his cheeky face.

Holding out his arm towards Jessica, she wrapped her arm in his and walked away with a broad smile on her face.

"I think they like each other," Zenny said to Turris.

"Yeah, that's good. I don't like the way Otto pays attention to you. Now he will have someone else to ogle."

"Oh stop it!" Zenny replied, "He was only being nice to me and nothing else. He's just that type of person."

"Well, I don't like it," Turris replied with gruff. Then a bit softer he added, "It's time to find out where you will be placed. Are you ready?"

"Yes!" Zenny answered, then added, "What I don't understand is why they need to place me. I don't mind working wherever they want me."

Turris answered as best as he could, "She's accepted for her beliefs and for the help that she can give us. But, for you it is different, you have a gift. Time wants us to free ourselves from our enslavement of the Mooncalves, and to hopefully make people aware of the incoming planetary systems or whatever is out there that is coming our way. Time wants us to change the foreseeable future. He wants us to know that we don't have to accept our planet the way it is. Time wants us to grow our consciousness to awaken the world to a possible loving future. And according to Timothy's report, you are different. You will need to talk to the elders for placement."

"Oh," was Zenny's simple response.

Walking into another room, she and Turris took a seat at the wooden table and waited for an elder to enter.

Chapter Twenty-Seven

Time was passing slowly for the two who were seated at the table. To break up the monotony, Turris and Zenny would, every so often, speak to each other in hushed tones. Anxiety began to creep in on Zenny, but she also sensed tension in Turris. Finally, Zenny stood up and started to pace around the room. Her footsteps caused a soft echo to reverberate throughout the quiet enclosure, even though she was walking lightly upon the hard wooden floor.

"Does it always take this long?" Zenny questioned, as she walked past Turris, then added, "Why did we come in here so soon, if they weren't ready for me?"

"I know it's hard to wait," he responded, "but sometimes, I wonder if that is a part of the test."

Not knowing how to react to his statement, Zenny said no more.

Fifteen minutes later, a voice sounded through the walls. Both Zenny and Turris were taken aback, for they thought they would see one of the elders enter the room.

"Turris," came the voice, "I will speak to Zenny alone. You may wait outside of the room, while she and I speak."

Turris rose as he turned towards Zenny saying, "This is highly unusual. But, don't fear. I will be right outside the door, if you should need me." Then he said into the empty room, "I don't question your motives, but this has never happened before." With that last comment, Turris left the room knowing he would not get a response.

Zenny's body began to tremble, as she started to feel a tremendous weight befall her supple body watching the door close behind Turris' large frame.

"Fear not young one," the voice came. "I need to speak with you privately." For a moment the voice stopped, then added; "You have been accepted for a special reason. We, the council and I, have found you to have some of the greatest gifts that have ever been bestowed upon one person."

For just a moment Zenny stopped hearing the words the voice was saying. She couldn't help but wonder what type of special gifts she had, and how she wouldn't have know that she had them, in the first place. She didn't feel special.

"Zenny?" the voice questioned, "did you hear what was said?"

Softly Zenny squeaked out, "No, I'm sorry I didn't. I was feeling the excitement of your acceptance and wondering what is so special about me."

"Thank you for your honesty," the voice responded, then continued, "I am to be called Luminary. You have a special gift. Something which is as strong as Emily had, when she was on the Earth. We feel you are prepared to do more than awaken people to the possible fore-told events. We have a specific task for you."

Zenny could feel her heart beat loudly in her chest, but she knew she must keep present in order to hear what the voice wanted of her.

"You are to infiltrate a mansion. You don't have much time to accomplish this for the time-line is consistently changing. You are allowed only three days to enter into the realm and seek the 'stone of consumption'. You need not bring it to us, you only need to view it and tell us about it."

"Please, if I may," Zenny interjected, "I have no knowledge of where the Mooncalves gather, nor do I have any idea, as to how I would become a part of their society within such a short time."

"You are *not* meeting with the Mooncalves. You are *not* infiltrating their society. You will be given limited directions and resources. This is some place much different, than you have ever experienced before. You will have Turris and Otto to take you to the place where you are to go," the Luminary said, with no inflection in its voice. "As we speak, the order is being given to your people. They are being informed of what is needed and what they are to do." Pausing he added, "Now look at the table and pick up what has been placed upon it."

Zenny looked down at the table and saw a burlap sack. Opening the sack, she saw the same opalescence orb which she had held in the void.

"Take the orb with you. When you need instruction or direction, look into it and ask your question. You will be given the answer. However," the voice warned, "you will not be allowed to bring it into the mansion with you, nor will you be able to ask any questions to the orb until after your safe return. So be certain that you ask what you think is important now, *before* entering the area. You will need to leave the orb in the flyer. But, do not worry about it being lost or destroyed, for the orb won't allow that to happen."

Amazed to see the orb and burlap sack, materialize out out nothing, Zenny placed her hands on either side of the object and gazed deeply inside the shimmering ball.

Looking around the vast emptiness of the room, Zenny said, "Please tell me to whom, am I speaking? Do you have a name other than the Luminary?"

———◉———

A LONG SILENCE PASSED, then the answer came, "This is Asher."

Zenny's knees became wobbly, as she tried to seat herself at the table, lest she fall to the ground and drop the orb. Placing the orb into its sack. Zenny breathed in deeply to calm herself.

Asher gave Zenny a few moments before he continued, "It's alright young one. There are special times, such as this where Father Time allows me to communicate with those upon Earth. And since this event has the possibility of wiping out *all* of the Earth, Time felt it necessary to give His people one last chance to repent before He destroys the world and starts it anew. The only thing that you may not do, is to divulge that it is I, Asher that spoke to you. You may call me Luminary to others, but you may *not* call me Asher to anyone else!"

Nodding her head in silent agreement, Zenny continued to listen to Asher as he went over the instructions to infiltrate the unspecified location.

A deep shift occurred while in the room. Zenny felt an urgency flow through her being. She knew she needed to awaken people to the upcoming events. She knew that this small group and she, must do whatever they could to help the people of the world change ... and change quickly!

Asher began to relate to Zenny all the things which were happening outside of the subterranean structure.

Idol worship, whether it be to a person or thing, must be slowed or stopped. People need to know that every action, whether it be good or bad, has an equal chain reaction elsewhere. The more good in the world, the better the world becomes, the more evil, the worse the world becomes.

At this point, in the history of the world, since most people are so engrossed in their viewing devices and watching their favorite performers, they lose track of reality. They want to emulate the controlled puppets. The performers vulgarly display themselves to the world in order to receive worship from the viewing audiences. They are willing to demean themselves, in order to please their own satanic idol in order to gain fame and popularity.

People are making themselves into freaks of nature, things that are unnatural. Most of the people who follow the performers programs, are carving their bodies into images that do not look human. They are applying pieces to their bodies that should never have been a part of a body. They look deformed and misaligned. They are turning their bodies into monstrous looking entities in order, to look like their favorite puppet performers, all of which don't know they are being controlled and manipulated behind the scenes, by the Mooncalves.

People are doing this all in the name of conformity and unity. However, what they don't understand that it is all a trick to deceive the people into becoming complacent and docile in order for the Mooncalves to completely control everything and everyone in their lives.

The Mooncalves have turned families against each other, in the name of protection. But what people don't know, is that none of what is being broadcast is real.[3] It is based in fear and not reality. They have people injecting substances that not only harm the human body, but change their DNA. And for those who do not inject the perverted substance, they then have the horror of watching their loved ones become something which is no longer human. They see their eyes glaze over and soon are taken from the living world and put into a place that is neither, here-nor-there. It is a place of complete manipulation and domination of the human soul. They become another puppet for the Mooncalves to control. For those who have injected, they do have the possibility of redemption. If their soul is strong. They will be able to remove themselves from its deadly grip, if they are willing to see the reality of their situation, which the Mooncalves would have over them. They can then be free to be who and what they should have always been; a free soul with incredible strength and power, rather than mindless beings walking the Earth.

The Mooncalves are creating a false sense of security. They are taking more control of every persons' lives, while removing even more of their freedoms which, at once time, all people had once possessed.

If not enough people change, then those who still possess free will, will need to prepare themselves for the possibility of incoming projectiles that may enter the planet. They need to arm themselves, they need to protect themselves from the possibility of turmoil caused by the losses of land and family. However, if Time feels that there are still good people on Earth, than He may choose to bring them to be with Him, rather having them live through the potential turmoil.

Finally, depending upon the crimes committed against humanity, people may experience either an ice-age or will be consumed by intense heat.

If you and The Sensitives are not able to change the billions of minds that are caught in the web of deception, then these are the things that may come to pass. If humanity can be saved then the world, and the good people upon it, will be spared the possible horrors to come. It is an enormous task that must be undertaken in order to save the world from mass destruction.

After hearing all that Asher was relating to Zenny, the young woman knew this was what she was meant to do. She wanted to help *The Sensitives*. She wanted to help the people of the world to see the truth. She wanted to try to turn the world in the correct direction. She wouldn't give into tyranny. Zenny knew she would fight for peace. She would do as Asher requested of her.

Chapter Twenty-Eight

Nearly two hours later, Zenny emerged from the room.

Standing outside the door, just as he said he would, Turris was waiting for her.

The moment Turris saw Zenny leave the room, he pulled her into a strong embrace. "I don't know what was said in there, and I know you are not allowed an answer, so just know that I will help you in any way possible."

"Thank you Turris," Zenny said softy into his ear, feeling great warmth emanating from his strong body. She needed the feeling of his body next to hers in order to comfort herself, and not feel as if she were in this fight all alone.

The things which Asher had told Zenny, were quite alarming and disturbing. Needing to feel another human being next to her, she pulled herself even further into his welcoming body.

Talking softly, Turris began to tell Zenny about what had been taking place while she was speaking with the Luminary in the room. "An order was sent to the main room from someone called the Luminary. There has been much speculation as to the name of the Luminary, but it is only speculation. We have never had an order that has come to us in such an unusual way. But not only that," Turris took in a breath and continued, "with you being a new recruit, some people wonder if there is favoritism going on. I, myself, don't understand that concept, but ... anyway, something has changed in the atmosphere. Some of the people are feeling anger towards your assignment. They also, feel perhaps that you shouldn't be here. I will not question you, as to who, or what, it was that you were speaking with, but there will be others who might try to get that information from you. If they try, just be firm and do not waver. It could make the difference between completing what is asked of you, or the possibility of failing."

Leaning into his chest and hearing the steady beat of his heart, Zenny said, "I understand. It was also, stressed to me *very* strongly, not to tell certain things about what took place inside the room. I *will* do as I was asked."

Walking down the hall hand-in-hand, the two met up with Otto and Jessica. Jessica was beaming, for she and Otto were getting along quite well.

Otto called out, as the two approached, "When do we leave?"

Jessica turned to Otto saying with surprise, "You want to get rid of me so quickly. I thought we were getting along just fine."

"Oh no, Jessica, don't think that," Otto answered quickly, "this has nothing to do with you and I. It has to do with the orders I was just given while you were out of the room."

"Oh, I see," Jessica replied feeling a little bit hurt, "I didn't know that I would be left out in the dark on everything."

"Don't say that," Otto replied softly, "you aren't going to be left out on everything, just the things that don't pertain to your duties. And when I am able to tell you about it, I will. But, for now it's important to keep things quiet." Adding with a loving embrace," Otto said, "I want you to know that even though we will be apart for a just a few days, I will be thinking of you. Will you be doing the same?"

Leaning into his stocky frame, Jessica replied, "I will wait for you and I will most certainly be thinking about you, *often*. I will also do as instructed." Pausing for a brief moment, she continued, "This has all come together so fast, it's hard for me to comprehend everything that is happening."

"I understand," Otto replied, then said, "you know you can't go home, anymore, don't you?"

"I know, but that's okay," looking deeply into his light blue eyes, she said, "I have no one there of importance."

Zenny heard Jessica's last comment and smiled to herself, knowing that she no longer cared for Keen.

"Jessica, I'm sorry to interrupt," Turris said kindly, "but we need to keep getting things done. So, I will need to take Otto from you. But, don't worry. We will be back in a few days time."

For a short distance the four walked together until Jessica left to help ready the air flyer.

After Jessica left, Turris turned towards Zenny saying, "you need to get your rest. After everything is ready, someone will come and get you."

Zenny nodded, and happily left going on her way to her new living quarters.

Chapter Twenty-Nine

By the time everything was ready, it was night. This was beneficial, for under the cover of darkness, it would be much easier to slip through the areas which were normally harder to pass. The Mooncalves, kept a close watch on everything with their self-manned mini flyers, and now was not the time to make a mistake.

AN HOUR BEFORE THEY were ready to leave, Jessica was tasked to wake Zenny from her sleep and to be certain that she was well fed before leaving.

Jessica knocked upon the slightly open door.

Feeling fully refreshed, Zenny called out, "Come in."

Jessica entered the barren room and told Zenny it was time to awaken and that she should get something hearty to eat. The two women walked to the food hall together, there they saw Otto and Turris sitting at a table with their food. They joined the men after they picked out their food. An hour later the trio were ready to leave, but Jessica was left behind, as instructed. As they began their flight, Zenny asked the orb to direct them to the area where they were to land. Then she asked it, where she was to enter the building.

The two men looked at the strange object in Zenny's hands, but said nothing, for they knew that if they were to know about the object and its uses, Zenny would tell them. They knew they were'nt to ask questions. Besides if they did, Zenny wouldn't be able answer them.

Chapter Thirty

Quietly, the air flyer landed on a large hill overlooking a very ancient dilapidated, massive estate.

Exiting the flyer, Zenny said, "There is no need to worry about me," trying to calm their fears and her own. "I should only be gone for a day or two; three days maximum. At day three, you will be given instructions from the orb as to where you are to pick me up." A nervous smile spread across her quivering lips as she spoke. "I will be leaving the orb and the sack in the flyer."

Turris's protective nature towards the young woman pulled strongly at his troubled mind. He would have rather have him do the task, but he knew that, that was not to be, so he said nothing. With one last hug and "good-bye" from both of the men, they watched as Zenny's body began to fade into the inky blackness, becoming a mere speck in the distance. Reaching for the binoculars, Turris kept a lookout on the young woman.

An hour later, Zenny arrived at the entrance of the structure looking a bit disheveled and panting from the arduous hike over the mountain. Knowing what was to be done, she had run the last half mile intentionally, so it would help with the deception which she must do in order to gain entrance into the mansion.

Knocking lightly upon the over-sized wooden door. Zenny heard foot steps approach, but not from inside, they were coming from the outside.

A rough hand grabbed her shoulder and yanked her around. She was standing face to face with a shadowed man. From what little she could see in the inky blackness, the man didn't look human, but it could also be just her mind playing tricks on her.

Zenny heard him say, "What are you doing here? This is private property. How did you get here?"

Beseeching, Zenny looked at the dark outline of the man and replied, "I was pushed out of a car. I asked a man if he would give me a ride home, but he didn't. Instead he took all my money, then he threw me out of the car."

"Don't you know it's not wise to ride with strangers?" came the deep menacing voice.

"I didn't really have a choice, my supposed friend dropped me off in the middle of nowhere, so she could be with her boyfriend and she left me on the side of the road," Zenny replied in a fearful voice.

A deep reverberating laugh echoed in the valley walls as the man said, "Come with me."

The man didn't know that her real fright came from the unearthly man who had hid in the shadows and surprised her with his presence.

Entering into the building, Zenny's eyes took a moment to adjust to the bright light.

The shadowy man who, Zenny could now tell was dressed in all black, said, "Wait here."

With a smooth, effortless stride, the man appeared to drift down the long hall and out of sight.

Chapter Thirty-One

What seemed to be several minutes later, were in reality, only moments. Zenny finally saw a woman walking down the hall. Her long green gown flowing across the marbled floor as she walked.

"Hello miss," the woman said greeting Zenny. "How did you get to my little hide away in the mountains?" she questioned Zenny suspiciously.

"I was thrown out a a car after a man robbed me of all my money," Zenny replied feeling her body tremble inside.

The tall woman noticed Zenny's quivering body and asked, "Are you cold?"

Zenny replied, "No, I'm just afraid. I've never been in this situation before and it frightens me," Zenny replied honestly.

"I see," the woman continued with suspicion still in her voice. "Well, I won't let you sleep out in the cold tonight. So for now, you will be given a guest bedroom, but . . ." the woman said with great authority, "you are *not* to come out of the room for any reason." Looking at her uninvited guest, the woman added, "The room which you will be staying in has an attached toilet, so you won't need to leave for that issue. However, if you need anything more than that, you are to pick up the phone and someone will help you. Do you understand?"

"Yes, ma'am. I am grateful for you hospitality," Zenny replied.

The woman seemed to like this answer and gave Zenny a brief smile as they walked down the long hallway.

Upon reaching a door, the tall woman said, "My name is Helena. You are a temporary guest of mine, and as such you are to follow my rules."

Zenny nodded, not really understand why the woman had to reiterate her warning, but she took it to heart and stayed in the given room for the night.

Chapter Thirty-Two

Morning came, Zenny was famished, but stayed in her room. When the light from the sun reached high in the sky, Zenny thought that someone would have already come by and told her it was time for her to go, but that didn't happen. Hunger was gnawing at her stomach, but still she waited. When noon came, Zenny picked up the phone receiver hesitantly, and heard a man's voice on the other end saying, "How can I help you?"

"I was wondering when I will be told that I may leave this room and go home?" Zenny questioned the faceless man.

"That is not up to me to decide. In the mean time, do you wish to eat something?"

"Yes please, I'm famished," Zenny replied.

"Why didn't you ring earlier?" came the icy reply from the man.

"I thought that I would be released for my room by now," Zenny replied with a bit of exasperation.

"You are not a prisoner," he replied with a hint of irritation in his weathered voice, then continued, "When your host comes to you, that is when you may leave," the man stated firmly. "Now what would you like to eat? Breakfast, lunch, or a snack?"

"Whatever is easiest," Zenny answered the man.

"Since it's past breakfast and lunch won't be served for another hour... and you seem unwilling to give me a set answer... I will have a snack brought up to you."

After his final words the man hung up with no more words spoken.

Speaking out loud, Zenny said, "Wow! That was rude." Realizing that she must be careful with her thoughts, actions, and especially her words, Zenny said nothing more.

An hour later there was a knock upon her door. Walking over to answer the door, Zenny looked out and saw no one around. Looking on the ground outside the door, was a tray of food, which had been left for her. Zenny picked it up and quietly closed the door. She stopped the urge of looking around at her surroundings beyond the door, for she knew she was being watched.

Several hours later, night fell. Zenny had yet to find out when she would be able to leave. She knew that her goal was to become a part of this place, but she couldn't stop the uneasy feeling which consistently flowed through her body. She felt, as if, pure evil dwelt within these walls. Though the building was immaculate, there felt a filth in the air. It felt demonic and bloody.

Chapter Thirty-Three

Around midnight, there was a knock upon the bedroom door which Zenny occupied. Rising from the bed, for she really hadn't been asleep, Zenny opened the door.

Helena said pleasantly, "Good-evening. How was your day?"

Zenny looked bewildered at the woman who was dressed in a long flowing blood red, gown. Her face was painted with deep red lipstick. Her hair was honey-blond. Her eyes were dark as chocolate. Taking in her long thin fingers, she noticed the oddness of her nails. They didn't seem quite right. They were painted black. There was a thickness about them. They almost appeared claw-like. But, certainly it just must be the lighting.

With a quivering voice Zenny finally replied, "I appreciate your hospitality, but I don't think I should burden you any longer."

"Oh you're no burden, child. In fact I would like for you to meet someone," Helena said with cool deliberation.

Another quivering wave coursed through Zenny lithe frame, but putting on a brave face, she replied, "I am a guest in your house. You took me in and fed me after I had been thrown out of a car. I am indebted to you. Out of courtesy, I will oblige you."

"Well stated my dear," Helena replied with a wide litigious grin.

The two women left the room. It felt good to be out of her forced confines.

As Zenny walked down the long marbled hall with Helena, she was thinking about the orb, wishing that she would have been able to bring it with her during this task. However, she knew for her mission to work, it would had to stay with Turris and Otto.

Raising her voice, in order to get Zenny's attention, Helena said, "My dear child what *are* you thinking about so intently? Surely you have been treated well during this short time you've been my guest."

"Oh, I'm sorry Helena," Zenny replied a little too quickly, "I was just thinking back to what happened to me the night before." Zenny hoped her lie would cover up her error of thinking of the orb.

"I see," Helena replied with bitterness, and hostility in her voice. "Perhaps, you *don't* appreciate my hospitality."

"Oh no! Please excuse my thoughts. It's just been such a long day," Zenny said in a hurried tone. "All I've done all day, is sit in the bedroom with nothing to occupy my thoughts, except for thinking about what had taken place prior to my being here."

Zenny's words seemed to appease Helena, for the tall woman allowed the issue to be dropped.

Having barely skated by her error, Zenny felt that this woman might have the ability to read her mind, and if not, then she had the ability to detect when things were a bit *off*. Either way, Zenny now knew better. And instead of thinking of the two men that were waiting for her at their post and the orb, Zenny decided to pay attention to her surroundings. For now, this was all she had. She needed to stay in the present and not think about the past or she might not be able to continue on with this ruse. It just all seemed like such a long time ago and so far way, but Zenny couldn't figure out why she felt that way.

Chapter Thirty-Four

Minutes later as Helena and Zenny continued to walk the long vast hallways of this exquisite building, Zenny heard Helena's voice cut deeply into her thoughts as she said, "Come, come child. Your mind appears to be elsewhere."

"I'm sorry Helena," Zenny replied, coming up with a viable excuse, "I'm just taking in all the grandeur which this building possesses. The outside, does not do justice to such beauty inside."

"Ah, yes. That is the way it is meant to be," Helena said matter-of-factually, "I don't want people snooping around here. I like my privacy. I forget what grandeur this old building holds for someone new, for its been a long time since I've had company."

Gesturing with her hand, Helena escorted Zenny into a very large room, momentarily forgetting her anger.

The only item in the room was a huge globe-shaped marble ball directly in the center. There appeared to be some sort of liquid flowing over the ball. The liquid appeared to be flowing around the ball as it recirculated its contents.

Seeing the huge object, Zenny visibly trembled as she unknowingly said out loud, "What is that?"

Helena smile deviously, saying, "Are you frightened child?

"A little, yes," she responded.

"It's good that you are aware of your feelings. It may keep you alive at some point," Helena said in a nondescript voice. Looking at the visibly shaken young woman, Helena said, "This is a man that I want you to meet. He has been my companion for quite some time. But, unfortunately he is no longer in human form and all I can do is look at his essence as it flows around the globe."

Unintentionally, backing away from Helana, Zenny replied, "I don't understand."

"You, will in time. But, until then, *he* is only to be known as the 'stone of consumption'. If anyone finds out that this ball is a human being, then I'm afraid that the person who told of my little secret, will have to die."

No light came from Helena's chocolate-brown eyes. Her presence appeared to enlarge as she gently put her hand on the marble ball and allowed the odd silvery liquid caress her hand.

Feeling a sense of renewal, Helena said in an almost seductive way, "You do not need to fear me, for I have what I need from him – well mostly. There are some times that I need extra sustenance from the outside, but I have people who usually take care of obtaining my required liquid. It's quite expensive and its price just keeps going up, but that is neither here-nor-there. What I really want is a human for a companionship. I am thinking of having you join me... here." Looking around at her mansion sized home, Helena added, in a tone befitting royalty, "I would like to see if you are my equal. I have been waiting a long time for someone to enter my life. It appears to be you. I just didn't expect for the person to literally walk into my life. But, here you are." Helena continued as she watched the color drain from Zenny's youthful face, "It's been a long time since I have felt comfortable with a human. The last human that I became close with... well, he didn't seem to appreciate my talents. If I remember right, his name was Jacob. But again, that's neither here-nor-there, for it was such a long time ago."

Zenny began to put the puzzle together. She wondered, "Is *this the woman named Helena, who was Jacob's past friend, from when Asher and Emily were alive on Earth. But how could it be? How could she still be alive and existing here on Earth, when all the others were in the heavens helping Time?*"

Wanting to keep Zenny in a state of shock and fear, Helena continued on, not knowing that Zenny had regained her senses.

Now it was Zenny's turn to listen intently. For now, was the time, that her objective was in hand and she wanted to remember as much as possible, so she would be able to inform Asher after she returned.

Hearing the obsessed woman's ranting Helena continued, "I loved him so, but he didn't love me in return. He loved another, but she was out of his reach and no where to be found. But, he didn't care, he would not give up is love for her. So, now is *my* time to make the world feel the pain which I felt all those years ago."

Pretending as though, she were in a trance-like state, Zenny neared the globe-shaped object, trying to get the woman to change the subject, so she would keep talking about the globe. "It looks so inviting," Zenny said in a soothing tone. Reaching out her hand as if to touch the silvery flowing liquid.

Helena quickly stopped Zenny from touching the 'stone of consumption.'

"You're not ready for that yet, my child," Helena said in a motherly tone. "Soon you will know all. Let's continue to walk and I will tell you more."

A sense of smug satisfaction coursed through Helena's veins, feeling, as if she had pulled Zenny into her fold.

"How do you get your food?" Zenny questioned, wanting to know, as much as, she possibly could before she left this filthy place.

Rubbing her hands together in a perverse sense of triumphant, Helena said, "Oh child, what a beautifully, wonderful question. Let me see, as I stated earlier, I have someone I can send out to do my bidding, but there is more to it than that. So, where do I begin?"

Seeing Helena's near child-like giddiness, made Zenny sick to her stomach, but she said nothing and waited for the vile woman to continue.

"Let me tell you a little bit about myself. That will help you understand better," Helena said licking her ruby red lips.

Zenny noticed that as the tall woman licked her lips, the fluid which she had used to redden them, appeared to flow back over her mouth and down her throat. Zenny heard Helena swallow the liquid with deep satisfaction. Trying had to keep herself from vomiting, Zenny desperately wanted to remove herself from the woman. She couldn't stand the thought of being around her, but she knew she must endure.

Entering another large room, Zenny focused here attention upon the vials upon vials of liquid placed in bottles upon the massive walls.

Looking at some of the vials which were at eye level, Zenny noticed names and dates written upon the bottles.

"What are these?" Zenny questioned.

"These are my prize possessions. This is how I live," Helena replied.

Zenny said, "I don't understand."

"Ohhh, this is the fun part," Helena said, nearly squealing with delight. "You see every few hundred years, I need to go out into the world and find a mate. Then I reproduce, I eat my young, which is usually twins or triplets, then I am able to live a long life. But, you see," Helena said as she took one of the vials in her hand and gently caressed it. "This are my snacks, in between feeding, you might say."

Holding the vial out to Zenny, and placing it in her trembling hand, Helena let out a loud cackle sounding laugh. Zenny nearly dropped the bottle. But, knowing what she was holding in her hand, gave Zenny the ability to hold firmly onto its contents.

Placing the vial back on the shelf, Zenny questioned the woman, but not really wanting to know the answer, yet needing to have Helena keep giving her as much information as possible, the young woman asked, "What are the names and dates on the bottles for?"

"Mmm, I like your questions," Helena responded becoming aroused, as she continued to look at the vials. Pointing at all the writing on the bottle, Helena began smoothly, "This is the name of the donor, and this the the day they were born." Sliding her thickened black nail over the writing, she continued, "this ... this is the date of their death," she said as she smacked her red lips together, as if she could taste its confines.

Zenny made a coughing sound, for she once again had to hold back the bile she was feeling in her throat.

Helena laughed, "Are you getting hungry, my dear? Does the thought of the vials make you thirsty and excite you? Can you feel the power emulating from this beautiful liquid?" Helena appeared to be in a world of her own as she continued on. "As you can see, my dear, this one, it's not very old. But, that is the way it must be, for any donor over the age of ten is no good to me. When I was out on my own and I didn't dwell in this place, I would keep some live ones. That way I could use the older ones for breeding purposes, so they were able to provide me with fresh essence and sometimes meat, whenever I liked." Looking away wistfully, Helena added, "Ah, but that was back then, and now I must rely on the Mooncalves to fulfill my needs. Since I'm confined to this prison for another century or more, I had to find a way to get my supplies. It's amazing how accommodating a huge conglomerate will be when they are offered the right price."

Fearing the answer, Zenny asked, "What was their price?"

Helena let out her cackling laugh once more, "Why eternal youth, of course. And for those that it doesn't work for, or for those that want to show the world that they age, well then they are cloned and reborn at a later date. Very simple really, but that is the boring stuff. Now let me finish," Helena said impatiently. "Time said I will be released in one more century or more. He thinks that I will have learned my lesson. But, it didn't work before, and it won't work this time either."

Taking in a deep breath, Zenny had to forcefully think of something else, anything else, which would temperately take her mind off the horrific images, which were coursing through her mind. Trying to change the subject, even if only for a moment, Zenny said, "Why is there so much here, surely you cannot go through this much in such a short period of time."

Glaring at Zenny through formidable eyes, Helena nearly roared, "You have no idea what it's like to be locked in this prison, with nothing to do, no one to turn to ...." Looking intently at Zenny, Helena said, "But, I *have* you now!" A perverse gurgling laugh, bubbled up from deep within her stomach and out her throat. Her lips flowed with red liquid. Drops fell to the hard marble floor, as she eagerly licked up its essence. Running her hands over the sides of her silky, crimson dress, she lovingly caressed her belly. Smug satisfaction coursed through her veins.

Physically jumping back out of the woman's reach; for a moment Zenny thought that perhaps she was Helena's next meal, but then she remembered that, that was not what Helena wanted from her.

"Oh you poor child, I won't hurt you. I want *you* to be a part of all this," she said as she gestured broadly with her arms. "You too, can live forever. We can enter a new age. We can rule with an iron fist. We can rule all of humanity, including the Mooncalves!"

Needing to make amends, Zenny said softly, trying to hide her tears and terror, "I don't think I can live up to your expectations."

"Oh nonsense, *I'll* teach you my ways. I know you're the right one for me. I feel that we fit together perfectly. Yes, you're a little bit rough around the edges, but ..." looking Zenny up and down, Helena added, "I will fix that problem very quickly. You are highly intelligent and I know you *will* learn quickly."

Temporarily haven taken the satanic woman's mind off of the vials, Zenny could feel Helena's next words before she even said them.

Grabbing a bottle from the shelf, Helena continued, "See these words; yellow, black, white, brown, albino, pink, tan, etcetra? That is the color of their skin. Do you know why that's important?" Helena questioned.

Giving a shake of her head as her answer, Zenny tried hard not to run from the room in horror. Firmly planting her feet in place, she needed to stop the overwhelming sense of being trapped. The young woman felt, as if, she were in a web with the spider nearing ever closer, seeing it begin to wrap its prey in a silken web of death.

"They each have their own taste. And each has different, shall we say, medicinal properties." Helena laughed as her use of words and continued on, "Some are better for instant relief, fertility, smoothness of the skin, reverse aging ... well you get the idea. I must say, "she added in hushed tones, "the most rare, most expensive are the albinos'. They are so good, for so many things."

This time Zenny saw Helena shudder, not because of fear or cold, but from ecstasy. Zenny knew she wasn't dealing with a normal human being, but it didn't stop the hatred that she felt for this woman standing next to her. Zenny knew she had to be careful with her emotions, for she didn't want Helena to know how she felt. For if she found out, Zenny wouldn't have much time left on this Earth and would have failed to complete her task and would have failed to help save humanity.

Zenny came back to the present as she listened to Helena say, "So as you can see, this is like my apothecary. It's just filled with all sorts of goodies!" Abruptly Helena changed the subject as she touched Zenny on the shoulder drawing the younger woman's attention to her words, "How do you feel about exotic foods?"

Trying to sound nonchalant, as she tried to keep the bile down that was dangerously lingering in her throat, Zenny replied honestly, "I don't really know, I've never had the money to try much of anything except the regular items that appear in the stores by my house."

"That's a pity. I will show you what you've been missing." Helena once again began to ramble on, as if, she no longer had her facilities about her. "I've only had my staff to keep me company, but now that you're here, I think I will keep you for quite a long while and teach you all that I know! We can rule together, hand-in-hand as one."

Feeling a chill run through her body, Zenny squeaked out feeling, as if, a cocoon was wrapping its threads tightly around her body, securing her in place, "What do you mean, *keep me here for quite a while?* I thought I was to be your apprentice, not your prisoner."

Without missing a beat, Helena replied, "I've been alone too long, but now you're here and apparently, you really have no one to go home to so, I think it's best for you to stay with me and I will teach you things that will help you out for our future together."

Helena's words were beginning to echo into Zenny's mind. She heard the satanic woman saying, "I will show you the things that I enjoy. You will learn to love the baby softness of flesh which has been prepared to perfection. You will learn to enjoy the pleasures of the flesh of men, who are neither living nor are they dead. You see, I know how to keep them in a state of limbo. I realized that after Jacob left me so he could be with that *witch* Emily, I understood that I hadn't learned what I should have. Way back then, I let my feelings for a human control me. *Not Any More!*" Helena boomed, "*You will* learn to be just like me and when the time comes, *you will* carry on my work. In time you will earn my trust and you will have more freedom. But, I must have complete compliance from you and you must never betray me, for you see, I can become enraged much more quickly than I used to. Being here, is such a terrible punishment. I'm just fortunate that the Mooncalves keep me supplied with the *things* I want and need. On rare occasions they supply me with someone for dinner," a small titter of laughter crossed the woman's deep red lips, "but you see they never last very long."

Zenny's brow furrowed as she tried to put out of her mind the meaning of *"supply me with someone for dinner"* and the double meaning of, *"never lasted very long,"* but the ominous words wouldn't leave her overwhelmed mind. She felt sick to her stomach, but she kept her thoughts to herself. Desperately, she wanted Helena to change the subject.

Carefully Zenny interjected into the older woman's ranting, saying, "You said that you haven't had many visitors, so why don't you send one of your staff to town, so you are able to have more guests?"

An almost hysterical laugh escaped Helena's lips, "They are only able to leave here to replenish my food stock and nothing more. When I tried to have one of my staff bring me a guest, he immediately disintegrated into dust the moment he arrived at the border of my land. And, well ... my guest ran away. So you see we are all trapped here."

"Am I trapped too?" Zenny questioned fearfully.

"No, you just aren't allowed to leave until I say, for you are from this current world, so you may return to your world. But, we must stay here no matter what happens out there. Even if the world ends, we will be stuck here until my punishment is done. I can keep you safe here with me and then you won't have to suffer the consequences of the the stupid beings out there."

Feeling a sudden need for sleep, Zenny almost begged Helena as she said, "I am exhausted. Would you please excuse me? I would like to go to my bedroom."

Triumphant washed over Helena as she knew her plan was working. She was manipulating Zenny to the point of no return. All she needed to do was to continue her barrage of words and images and soon Zenny would be hers to mold like putty in her nimble hands.

"I will walk with you," Helena said as she guided Zenny by the shoulder. The older woman wanted to have Zenny to dream of her, and all of her all her unholy material possessions, before sleep. She wanted the child to only remember what she implanted within the young woman's subconscious mind.

Absently agreeing, Zenny walked dazed along the halls and corridors back to her bedroom.

Chapter Thirty-Five

Waking to the third morning, in the small camp that Turris and Otto had set up, Turris stretched his long body in the sleeping bag which was laying on the tent's hard ground. Looking around the tent, he listened to Otto as he snored in his sleep.

Rising to the brightness of the day, Turris exited the tent and began to make breakfast. The concerned man vowed that by nightfall, if Zenny hadn't returned, then he would begin the trek to the old mansion in the valley below. He knew he would have to bring reinforcements, such-as fire arms which were specifically meant for unnatural beings and entities.

As Turris' mind went into the future, several minutes later, he heard Otto lift the flap of the tent he was sleeping in, and then close it behind him.

Otto's words caught Turris off guard as he heard, him say, "I thought I could smell the aroma of coffee and pancakes."

Looking up from the small campfire, Turris replied in a teasing tone, "Well at least something can wake you up. I wasn't certain if I would have to come in there an make you get up."

"Nah! Just had a restless night. I was thinking about Jessica. That woman seems to have a hold of me. Something that I'm not used to. She just seems too good to be true."

Turris teased, "Are you telling me *you're* in love?"

Nodding his agreement, Otto said, "Sure feels like it!"

Grunting, Turris added, "Well after we get Zenny home, you will be able to be with Jessica again. So, how about you keep you mind on the task at hand?"

Hearing Turris's sudden change from teasing to harshness, Otto replied, "Hey man, I can still think my own thoughts as long as it doesn't interfere with our mission."

"That's the point!" Turris snapped back, "It is interfering with the mission, especially since you didn't get much sleep last night!"

"Who said I didn't get much sleep?" Otto rebuffed, then turned from Turris' site, so as not to spur an argument with the angered man. Otto knew there was no reasoning with his friend when he was in this state, so he dropped the subject.

The two men fell into a silent truce and allowed things to be as they were.

With the approaching noon hour, Otto felt Turris' impatience grow. Otto had all he could do to stop Turris from traipsing down the small mountain and bringing Zenny back.

"Come on my friend," Otto said as he watched Turris pace back and forth. "When the time comes, we will pick up Zenny."

"How are we to know when the time comes?" Turris reproached.

Walking the few steps to the tent, Otto pulled out the burlap sack which contained the opalescence orb, and said, "This is what will tell us when the right time is."

"What if it's too late? What if we can't reach her in time? We don't know what's going on down there!" Turris snapped at his friend.

"You need to calm yourself," Otto replied in a non threatening tone. "Try to think of this, as any other mission that we have been sent on ..."

"This is *not* just another mission!" Turris interrupted.

Looking at the tall man standing a few feet from him, Otto said in nearly a hushed tone, "Are you in love with Zenny?"

Seeing Turris suddenly stand erect, Otto nearly spit out the coffee that he had just taken a sip of.

Turris fell silent. A few moments later, he replied after much thought, "I think you're right."

Walking over to his friend, Otto carefully removed the binoculars from his hands, for the man had been, much too frequently, peering through the lens in search of Zenny.

Looking directly into Otto's eyes, Turris replied with almost a bitter sadness, "I didn't realize how much I cared for her, until now." Looking into the far distance, he added, "I think the next task, if it involves Zenny, I should not be a part of. I don't want to hamper what we are trying to do, just because of my feeling towards her."

"You know that is not how it works," Otto replied kindly to his friend. "You know that it is not up to us, who is sent on a mission. Besides," Otto continued, "maybe, this is part of our task. Maybe, it's to help you understand your feelings towards her."

An unknown anger, once again, washed over Turris as he replied, "I don't care how she was approved for this *mission, I* don't think she should have been sent. She's never had experience with people who are more than what they appear to be."

Placing a hand on his friend's shoulder, Otto tried to calm him. Turris' erratic behavior was concerning. Allowing time to lapse. Otto slowly walked away and sat on the hill, as he gazed out into the distance. Something seemed off. Things didn't feel right in this place.

Several minutes later, Otto stood and said, "I think there is something about this place that is corrupt."

Perking up from his stupor, Turris said, "What do you mean?"

Otto replied, "Since when do we act like two love-sick puppies?"

A flash of realization crossed through Turris' mind as he replied, "I see what you're saying." Looking through the binoculars, Turris suddenly understood, that though he did have feelings for Zenny, he knew those feelings were somehow being intensified while in this place. And perhaps that is what was also happening to Otto with his feelings for Jessica.

As a flash of understanding coursed though both men's bodies at the same time, they blurted out, " This place is satanic!"

With nearly a sigh of relief, they both felt a lifting, as if, someone had removed a curtain from their eyes showing them what was truly going on here. No longer were they under the spell of this place. Now they could see clearly.

Turris walked over to the orb and asked, "When should we pick up Zenny?"

The orb answered.

Both men felt stunned, they didn't think the orb would actually answer.

Chapter Thirty-Six

What seemed like only moments to Zenny had in reality been several hours. As her eyes cleared, she began to see light streaming through the heavily draped windows.

Looking around the room, Zenny was startled by seeing the presence of Helena at her bedside.

Feeling that this must be some sort of test, Zenny nonchalantly said, "What time is it?"

"It is late afternoon, my dear child. You have done well." Looking around the bright room Helena, said, "Come, it is time for you to receive the final initiation and then we will begin to take back my empire and return it to its fully glory." Looking wistfully and sighing, Helena added, "Like Sodom and Gomorrah."

Not having any memory of what transpired while she slept, Zenny was fearful as to what might have been done to her, or what she might have unknowingly done.

Seeing Zenny's bewilderment, Helena said, "Don't worry child, you're still pure in form, for that is the way it must be. However, over the next several days, you will come to enjoy the feeling of complete power without consequence. Then you will feel the overwhelming fulfillment given to you through the 'stone of consumption'. The feeling is exhilarating and nourishing.

Unintentionally, Zenny felt herself swallow when Helena said the word 'nourishing'.

Helena let out a deep laugh at the confusion she saw on Zenny's face. "You see my child, you are already beginning to conform to this place. It is giving you a thirst, for something which you have yet to taste." With superiority, Helena completed by saying, "I knew you were the one for me!"

Feeling a shiver pass down her spine and through her arms and legs, Zenny wasn't certain if she would be able to continue her task. How could she do what was needed? Her only solace came in the knowing that it had been three days, and perhaps the two men would soon come to extract her from this vile, soul-sucking environment and return her to the light. It couldn't come too soon. Zenny felt an odd pull for wanting to learn more. *Questioning herself, she thought, "Is it that I want to learn more, or is there some type of draw that makes me want to sample,* that which Helena has to offer me?" Her thoughts didn't sit well with her beliefs. *"Just hold on a little longer."*

Chapter Thirty-Seven

"What is it saying?" Otto questioned, as he heard the orb, but was not able to understand it's words.

"It is saying that under the cover of night, we are to remove Zenny from the premises and it said how it is to be done." Looking once again into the distance, Turris said, "I hope she can hold out until then." But in the back of his mind he was thinking, *"I need to free her now! Maybe, I should just take the flyer and go."*

The opalescence orb broke into Turris's thoughts as it called out to Turris, for only he was able to understand it words, *"You are to wait until night, any interference prior to that, could cause her more harm than good."*

"What did the orb say this time?" Otto questioned as he heard sounds coming from the orb.

Knowing the message was meant for only he, Turris said, "It's telling us to be ready for tonight and how we are to get Zenny."

Looking at his friend questionably, Otto said, "So how do we do it?"

Quickly replying, Turris said, "We are to take the flyer to a certain open area in the mansion at 3 a.m. and lift her out with the collapsible ladder."

"Is that all?" Otto questioned incredulously.

"It should be an easy extraction, as long as Zenny is able to get to the site in time."

Seeing a shift in Turris, Otto said, "What's troubling you? Something seems to have changed again.

"I can't stop this damn thinking," Turris burst out! "I know, that Zenny must have the capabilities to do this task, and the Luminary must feel that she is a wise and cautious woman, but this protective feeling won't go away. It's really beginning to nag at me." Turning towards the distant mansion, Turris mumbled, "I need to know what's happening. I can't take this feeling of fear."

"Don't you think that when we get off of this mountain, things will appear to be much calmer and more clear?" Then adding a second thought Otto said, "Why haven't you looked into her dreams or went to her while she slept? You could easily see what is happening to her, if you chose to," Otto commented innocently.

Glaring at his friend, Turris said much too gruffly, "Don't you think that if I was able to do that, that I would already have *done it!*"

Taking a step back, Otto said, "It was just a question," he replied in his defense. "So are you telling me, that in this place, you're unable to communicate with Zenny?"

Unconsciously, Turris put the binoculars up to his eyes, and answered, "This place seems to have taken that ability away from me."

Risking another outburst from the intent man standing near him, Otto questioned, "Do you mean to say the Luminary has stopped you from seeing into people's dreams?"

"No," Turris replied, "Not the Luminary, it's this place. "I am still able to enter other peoples dreams, but not Zenny's. Apparently, it seems like there is some kind of energy field protecting anything from the inside getting out; or perhaps anything from the outside getting in."

"Oh man, that must be hard," Otto remarked adding, "Remember we will back home soon, and then this place won't be able to influence our thoughts and judgments any longer."

Chapter Thirty-Eight

Rising from the bed, Helena said, "Take the rest of the day and explore my confines. I'll come to you again when it is time to feed."

Zenny's stomach began to churn hearing her words 'feed', but replied, "Will I be able to get some breakfast or lunch?"

"Of course, child," Helena replied as she picked up the receiver of the telephone. "What would you like?"

Zenny relayed her order.

After hanging the phone up, Helena said, "Have an enjoyable day, and I will see you later tonight!"

———◉———

THE DAY WORE ON MUCH too long for Zenny. Knowing she was under constant surveillance, didn't stop her from exploring, for she knew that, that is what Helena wanted her to do. But she also, understood that she had been given specific instructions as to which of the rooms she was not allowed to enter. As far as Zenny was concerned, that part didn't matter, for she was shown the 'stone of consumption' and *that* was the purpose of her coming to this satanic mansion in the first place.

Coming across one of the workers in the the hallway, Zenny was eager to talk to someone new to find out what she could about this place.

Smiling politely, Zenny said, "Hi, I'm Zenny. What's your name and what do you do here?"

The overly portly, ancient looking lady, turned around and said, "Uba ... cook."

Raising a brow, Zenny said, "Your name is Uba Cook?"

Shaking her beefy head, she replied, "Name is Uba. I am the cook."

"Oh, I see," Zenny said with a titter of embarrasment.

No smile came from the very elderly woman's lips, as she began to walk towards the kitchen.

"May I follow you?" Zenny questioned, as she came into step with Uba.

"Ain't for me to decide. Do what you feel is right for you."

Rather confused by her reply, Zenny followed Uba down the long hall. Turning left led them to the entrance of the kitchen. It was massive. It looked as thought it could easily serve several hundred people at one time.

"Oh my, this room is large!" Zenny said out loud. Taking in a enticing aroma of the food which was cooking upon the stove, Zenny commented, "Mmm, it sells wonderful!"

"Oh honey, you ain't tasted nothing, like what I cook!" Uba replied with a vile looking smile. "Would you like to see what I am serving up for dinner?"

"Oh yes. What I've had thus far, during my short stay here, has been tasty," Zenny replied happily.

"It looks like baby pig," Zenny replied as she peered into the large pot.

Hearing the cheerfulness and seeing the pleasing smile cross Zenny's lips, Uba responded with untethered enthusiasm, "This ain't no baby pig."

Seeing an odd slithering movement flow over Uba's deeply wrinkled body, Zenny visibly shivered. Not wanting to draw attention to her unease, she said, "I suppose I should let you tend to your cooking. I will continue my tour."

"Yup! Good idea," Uba replied not paying attention to Zenny for Uba was already continuing to work on the meal.

After Zenny left the room, she knew she was unable to take a deep breath to calm herself for Helena would be watching. Instead, she walked quickly down the hall and out into the courtyard. Looking up into the clear sky, she wished that it was already 3 a.m. For last night she was told that would be the time that Turris and Otto were to come to her with the flyer. She was also, told her she must be to meet them.

Chapter Thirty-Nine

It was nearly 2 a.m., as Zenny rose from her bed. She had taken a nap in order to be prepared for tonight's, events, including her release from this place. She felt a bit more refreshed, but still the heaviness of the atmosphere hung thickly in the air. It felt suffocating and filled with such deep hatred that it made Zenny feel at times, as if, she were choking. It was hard to want to be in such a vile place, but she new that she had to continue with the farce. She couldn't let Helena know that all she wanted to do, was leave this place and be rid of Helena's toxic presence. Yet, there was still that nagging feeling in the back of Zenny's mind, that she would like to stay just a little longer.

Deciding to have a stroll around the courtyard, Zenny admired the well trimmed trees and neatly planted flower and vegetable beds, outside of the confines, made it easier for her to breathe. But, even there, the heaviness of the air was thick with a demonic presence.

Over half an hour passed. The thrill of going home, was beginning to pull strongly at Zenny's mind. It was almost 3 a.m. as she began to begrudgingly re-enter the mansion. Zenny knew she needed to show her presence one more time before going back outside. So she decided to stroll over to the kitchen. As she neared the door, she heard a loud explosion, then saw flames licking the sides of the long hall, which she had just walked down. Zenny saw Helena running into the flames which were now pouring out of the kitchen. Just then, Zenny heard the flyer overhead. She was deeply relieved to know that soon she would be out of this wretched place.

Seeing the flames ferociously, grasping at her body as she turned around and began running back outside, Zenny knew she had to brave the flames, for it was the only way out of the building. She had to get to the courtyard. Bursting out of the outside door, she saw the flyer dropping a ladder to the area where she had been only moments before.

Turris and Otto's eyes were filled with deep concern as they saw flames ripping its way through the mansion. But their fears eased, as they saw Zenny swiftly run from the inferno and rush over to the ladder which hung from the flyer. Quickly, she latched onto the rung. With haste Turris drew up the ladder while the flyer continued on its way, out of the area.

Climbing into the flyer, Zenny heard Turris' deep sigh of relief saying, "I'm so glad you're safe. All I could do was think about what might be happening down there. Then I saw the explosion!" Looking at

Zenny to be certain she was well, Turris continued, "What happened? What caused the explosion? How did you get out of there? Were you hurt?"

Leaning her head softly upon Turris' shoulder, Zenny replied kindly, "I can only answer one question at a time." Sighing as relief washed over her heavily burdened body, she continued, "I'm so exhausted."

Taking a deep breath, Turris said lovingly, "Are you alright?"

"I'm fine," Zenny replied.

"What caused the explosion?"

"I don't know. I think *that* was the Luminary's distraction, so I would be able to leave unheeded. I'm glad that you were so close by. It made easier to get away," Zenny said with great relief.

Otto chimed in, "We've been circling the area for over half an hour. Not in their field of vision, but close enough, so we could be here quickly."

Turris blushed, as he said with a shakiness in his voice, "I wanted to be certain that we could get to you as soon as possible."

Zenny smiled, lifting her head briefly from Turris's shoulder saying, "Thank you."

Looking towards Otto who was piloting the flyer, Zenny said, "Thanks Otto. I really appreciate the quick escape. I must say, that I didn't know how the timing would work out, but I'm glad it did."

Zenny heard the relief in both Turris and Otto's voices. She too, was quite happy to be removed from the putrid area.

Both men wanted to ask many more questions, but they knew that Zenny was told not to speak of the task to anyone, unless the Luminary told her she could. So, the two men didn't questioned her further.

Chapter Forty

When they finally landed at the subterranean village, Zenny was emotionally exhausted. Otto excused himself and told both Zenny and Turris, that he was going to see Jessica.

Zenny smiled, weariness showing in her face, as she said to Otto, "Would you let Jessica know that I'm fine? I'm certain she will be worried about me."

"Of course I will," Otto replied excitedly knowing that soon he would see the woman he was falling in love with.

Zenny began to walk to her room.

Turris called out, "Zenny, can I walk with you?"

Zenny nodded and Turris strode the few steps next to her.

Placing a protective arm around the top of Zenny's waist, the two walked down the hall in silence.

Entering her room, Zenny thanked Turris for walking with her.

Turris softly said, as he looked deeply into Zenny's depleted green eyes, "I was worried about you. I know that we haven't had much time together, but I want you to know that I have feelings for you."

A light blush crossed over the young woman's face as she replied, "I have feelings for you, as well."

Seeing the young woman's eyes begin to glow with warmth, rather than, the tiredness which was there only moments ago, Turris leaned in as Zenny lifted her arms and placed them around his neck. Turris wrapped his arms around Zenny's waist and the two gently kissed.

"Knock, knock," came the sound from the slightly opened door.

"Excuse me ma'am, you are requested in the Luminary's room. You are to be debriefed."

Zenny and Turris' embrace quickly ended.

Turning towards the young man Turris said, "She just arrived back. Can't she have a moment's peace?"

The younger man replied, "Sorry Turris, but the order didn't come from me."

"Order! Since when did things become an *order*?" Turris raised his voice as his ire shone through.

"Sorry, but those *requests* didn't come from me," the young man replied agin with a bit more insistence.

Zenny moved from Turris's side and walked over to the young man, as she said, "It's okay Turris. I'm fine. I'm certain that *he* probably just wants to hear my version of what had taken place."

"It could wait," Turris mumbled under his breath. "I'm know you're exhausted. It's nearly five in the morning!"

A half smile crossed Zenny's lips as she said to Turris, "I can sleep after I've spoken with the Luminary."

"I suppose there really is no choice for you? You have to do what is being called upon you. I just hope the Luminary makes it quick, for you sake." Turris commented with a bit too much gruff.

Zenny smiled at her defender, and followed the young man out of the room.

Chapter Forty-One

Nearly an hour later, Zenny emerged from the meeting with Asher. She was exhausted. Methodically, she walked to her room. She didn't notice all the staring faces as she walked down the hall. She was too exhausted to even care.

Without pulling the covers back or even trying to make herself comfortable, Zenny plopped herself upon the bed and fell instantly asleep. But, it was not a restful sleep. Her dreams were filled with all the horrors she encountered during her stay at Helena's.

Having a need to hide her emotions, feelings, and thoughts in order to keep them from being known to the evil woman, during her stay at the mansion, made Zenny's mind trap all those images, scents, and thoughts in her psyche. But, now that she was safe, all of it came flooding back to her during her dreams. But these dreams were so vivid, so real, it was as if, she were really living them.

Seeing dead bodies all around, Zenny pushed and struggled to get away, but she was being held down by an invisible web of silken steel-like fibers. One after another, their bodies were being discarded as their essence was being drained from them. Seeing the life-less images mercilessly tossed into a pit of fire, as the scent of charred flesh lingered in the air and filled her nostrils with its putrid scent.

Gagging from the smell, Zenny tried to scream out, but was unable to, for her mouth was covered by the web. Tears streamed down her face, as she tried in vane to free herself and help the innocent victims from being drained and then consumed by the blazing intensity of the fire.

Make it stop, her mind cried out in grief. But, nothing happened, nothing stopped. Then Helena walked into her dreams. The older woman began gathering energy to from the satanic marble globe, which oozed it life essence into her own being. Helena delighted in its being. Pleasure coursed through her body, as she grew ever-increasing in size. Soon her height was that of a giant. Her black nails grew even thicker and longer, resembling claws. Her face no longer held the form of a human. It had become warped and transformed into a creature which was so hideous, that even Helena would no longer look upon her own face. Any thing which container a mirror-like finish, was swiftly destroyed by her massive clawed hands. Cackling out with delight at her strength, caused the walls of her confines to crumble to the ground. She was free! She had been, waiting many centuries to be free. Free to go into the world and rend all the children into liquid mountains, to be consumed at her leisure. Devastation and havoc followed in her wake. All that was once beautiful and green, now just ash. All that was pure and good, vile and wicked.

NO ONE WAS IN ZENNY'S room to release her from her night terror. No one would be able to help her with the overpowering images which flowed effortlessly through her mind. She had to bear the pain and torment on her own. Her dream continued throughout the hours of her sleep. Endlessly, hearing the screams and pleas of people she had never met.

Chapter Forty-Two
"Boom!"

People began running to see where and what created the explosion. Zenny was finally, awoken from her tortured sleep. Springing out of bed, she too ran into the hallway to see what had happened.

As an older woman passed by her, Zenny called out, "What happened?"

"No one knows," the woman replied as she continued in the direction of the sound.

Zenny followed suit. She had continued her journey down the hall seeing smoke billowing from the water pump room. Water was flooding the area. Those inside the room we battling to control the flow and shut off the main valve.

Knowing that there was nothing she could do to help, Zenny stayed out of the way, as the people inside continued to try to stem the flow of water. Soon, the water stopped. People looked around, feeling bewildered.

As a hush passed over the people and things began to calm, Zenny asked one of the men that was leaving the room, "What happened?"

"I don't know," replied the man.

"I know the flow has stopped, but is there anything I can do to help?" Zenny questioned.

"Yeah, find out who did this," he answered.

"This wasn't an accident?" Zenny asked incredulously.

"No ma'am, this was no accident," the man replied as he began to walk away, not out of rudeness, but out of lack of answers.

Understanding the man's dismay, Zenny asked him no more questions. Instead she went in search of Turris.

WALKING THROUGH THE halls, Zenny searched for Turris. Numerous people passed by her, but none were the person she was looking for. She asked a few people that walked by, but none new where he was.

Resigning herself to the thought, that in time, Turris and she would meet up again, Zenny went to the dining hall and decided to have breakfast. She was famished, not only from her long night of night terrors, but also from the sudden shock of waking up to a loud boom.

Halfway through her breakfast, Zenny saw a familiar face, it was Jessica.

Smiling as her friend neared, Zenny said, "It's so good to see you!"

Jessica sat down next to Zenny. Concern entered her face as she questioned Zenny saying, "How are you doing? Did you sleep well? I was worried the whole time you were gone. Did you accomplish what you needed to?"

"I'm fine," Zenny replied. "I slept alright for it being the first night back." Looking into the distance, Zenny corrected, "Well I guess it was early morning when I arrived back, but you know what I mean," she said smiling to her friend. "Do you know what happened?" Zenny questioned Jessica about the boom sound.

Answering the question, Jessica responded, "It appears that no one knows what happened. I'm just glad that they were able to stop the water flow, otherwise we might have had to evacuate."

"The man in the water pump room, didn't think it was an accident. Have you heard anything about that?" Zenny questioned further.

"There's a rumor going around," Jessica said in a soft whisper, "that it was an inside job." Looking around to be certain that no one was paying attention to them, Jessica added, "apparently, they think is one of the new recruits."

"That doesn't make sense." Zenny replied, "The Sensitives screen the candidates before accepting them. So, how could something like this have happened?"

"According to Hugh," Jessica continued in her hushed tone, "it can happen and it did once before. It had something to do with, allowing someone to rise too quickly in their abilities and they used that ability against the group."

Looking puzzled, Zenny commented, "It just doesn't make sense." Zenny added, "Who's Hugh?"

Laughing to break the tension, Jessica replied, "He's a guy I work with. We were both recruited at the same time and we both do the tasks that are assigned to us." Adding, as if she were telling a secret, Jessica said, "He thinks the things we do are menial. But I think, that everyone has a job to do, and if they do it to the best of their ability, then it will create a harmonious work environment."

Zenny smiled, relieved that Jessica was being herself. It felt good to be around *normal* people with normal thought patterns, once again.

Chapter Forty-Three

"Rurrr, rurrr, rurrr!"

Both women looked up from the table with astonishment.

"It's another alarm," Jessica exclaimed!

"What's going on?" Zenny chimed in.

Many people jumped up from their seats at the tables and rushed over to the Visvoc communication system.

From their seated position, Zenny and Jessica could hear and see what the Visvoc was relaying.

"There's been another accident," came the woman on the screen. *"We have a chemical spill in level five. Those of you, who are adept in handling the situation, please come and provide assistance. All others, please keep your distance and allow the helpers to do their job. Thank you."* The message ended.

Some of the people who were listening; who were able to clean up the chemicals; ran to assist to help contain the spill. Other people began to walk towards the area to try to find of more of the distressing situation.

"This is really weird," Jessica said to Zenny. It's been so quite for such a long time and now we've had two accidents. I think something is going on."

Zenny responded, "This isn't right," she said shaking her head in disbelief. "Why do you think things like this are just happening now? I just came back from being in such a vile place and now I have to come to this and I don't even know what to do to help the situation."

"Don't worry about it Zenny," Jessica said reassuringly. "We will handle this. Perhaps you should just take a break and walk around the compound. Get some fresh area in the arena. The dome should be uncloked during this time of day and you will be able to see the sun."

Taking a deep breath, Zenny answered, "I think that is a great idea. I would really like to clear my head right now."

Both women stood from the table, Jessica hugged Zenny lightly and said, "try to relax. Everything will be fine."

Zenny nodded and walked to the arena.

Chapter Forty-Four

Entering the arena, Zenny breathed in deeply. Her thoughts began to clear as she walked around the area. Taking in the various trees and plants, helped to ease her over-burdened mind. Off in the distance, the young woman noticed the enormous garden beds. Leisurely walking to them, she allowed her nostrils to be filled with the wonderful aromas. Nearing the vegetable beds, her sight beheld the plethora of numerous plants, which were planted to feed the entire subterranean village.

Moving further on, she took in the various flowers and gently touched them with her outstretched hand. Even further in the arena, Zenny noticed a waterfall. Hearing the loud roar as she stood next to the fast flowing water, she reached out her hand and cupped it. Quickly, she brought the liquid to her lips and drank in the deeply soothing taste of the water.

Zenny's senses will filled with happiness and thoughts of peace. Not wanting to leave this refreshing place, the young woman sat on the ground next to the roaring waterfall. Leaning back on her elbows, she looked up through the dome. Taking in the bright sunlight of the day. She knew it wouldn't be much longer before the dome would have to be covered once again. When she first arrived, she was told that the dome needed to be covered by 5 p.m., For if it wasn't then the Mooncalves would be able to see the structure. Fortunately, for the people living below, angle of the dome kept it hidden during the hours of 10 a.m. and 5 p.m. This time period worked well, for it gave the growing vegetables enough light to be able to produce their crop properly.

As her mind drifted to calmer times, an alarm suddenly went off again. Zenny jumped up and ran over to the communications system. It was over two acres away, so she had to run fast in order to find out what the message said. Turning the device on, she listened to the newest announcement.

"It appears as though we have another incident at hand. Those who are able to help, please come to the food storage area. A fire has begun and is rapidly spreading. For the rest of you, please keep your distance. I will be making another announcement shortly. Thank you."

The voice stopped. Zenny walked out of the arena feeling dejected. There was such beauty here only moments but, now just a sense of fear clouded her thoughts. She couldn't understand what was happening. Then she thought out loud, "Asher! Maybe, he can help!"

With a lightened step, she ran to the intake room to try to make contact with Asher.

Chapter Forty-Five

"Asher! Asher! Please Luminary, please talk to me!"

Several minutes of silence passed, as Zenny waited to hear Asher speak.

"Why do you call for me, Zenny?" came Asher's annoyed voice.

"I'm sorry, but this is important," Zenny said feeling a tightness grow within her body. Then with a subdued tone she added, "Strange things have been happening since my return from Helena's. Please help us."

Silence wafted through the room as Zenny waited, once again, for Asher to speak.

"Lay on the couch and close your eyes," Asher's voice came with a rumble.

"What couch?" Zenny questioned as she looked around the room.

Spying a large couch against the back wall, Zenny replied, "That wasn't there before. How did you do that?"

"Are you going to question me, or do you want my help?" he responded as his irritation grew.

"I'm sorry," Zenny said contritely.

Walking over to the couch, Zenny layed down and closed her eyes.

"Be still," Asher demanded.

Several minutes later, Asher said, "You may rise."

Coming to a sitting position on the couch, Zenny questioned, "Do you know why so many calamities have been happening around here?"

Feeling affronted Asher responded, in anger, "Do you think I don't know how to do something so easy?"

Again, Zenny apologized as she said contritely, "Asher, I don't mean to question your abilities, I'm just concerned with the events that are happening."

Moments of silence filled the air. Zenny didn't know if Asher was doing this to make her feel uncomfortable or if he was thinking. She didn't speak a word as she waited for Asher's response.

"When I am done speaking, I want you are[4] to go to your room and stay there," Asher said brusquely as he continued, "Contact Jessica through your communications device. There will be instructions written down on a piece of paper, in your room, for you to read to Jessica. She will get the needed supplies and soon these things will stop occurring."

"Will you tell me what is causing these disasters ...?"

"Enough! Be gone!" Asher bellowed and said no more.

Swiftly Zenny left for her room. Upon entering, she saw a note laying on the table. Lifting it from the table she began to read:

Fine wire thread

Weave every five strands of Zenny's hair into the threads
Leave wires in hair until hair has grown out
When hair is long enough it may be cut

Zenny, Helena has put her essence into your hair strands, however, as they grow out, they can no longer do damage. After a hair falls out or is removed from your head, for the next two hours, the essence of that hair is able to transmit to Helena. She will be able to view all that is around that strand of hair.

If the hair lands on a person, it will continue to transmit the signal causing the person to do acts of destruction, which they would not normally do. That person is being controlled by Helena. A weak person has no control over Helena. They must be set apart from others until they have a strong Constitution once again or until two hours have passed. Helena is able to make the person do commit immoral acts. However, a strong person, on the other hand, is able to fight off the images and thoughts which are being placed in their minds. They know the difference between right and wrong. They have the ability to set strong boundaries in their mind and keep a proper perspective in regards to safety and goodness to others.

Chapter Forty-Six

Zenny called Jessica into her room and told her all about her meeting with the Luminary, however, not divulging his name. She also, showed the note to Jessica. Swiftly, Jessica began to do as she was asked.

While Jessica was braiding Zenny's hair, Zenny thought about how she was going to tell Turris about the events and why they were happening. She was worried that she would be cast out of the subterranean village and not be allowed back in, for fear of bringing some other sort of destruction to the area. She knew she would have to reassure Turris and the others, but she was uncertain as to how to do it.

Three hours had passed since the two women were together, they talked about many things, including how to tell Turris and the others, but they were unable to find a solution.

"Jessica?" Zenny asked quizzically, " Would you not mind telling anyone about this until I've had a good night's sleep? Maybe, I'll be able to come up with something by then." Pausing, she added, "No more damage will come to the village, for you have braided the wires in my hair." Looking down at her feet, she said with embarrassment, "I feel so stupid for allowing such a thing to happen."

Jessica touched Zenny's shoulder saying, "How could you have known? If what I've heard and been told about this Helena woman, she is pure evil and would do anything to create destruction and mayhem wherever she could." In a softer tone, she added, "Try to calm yourself and get some sleep. It's over now."

Smiling at her friend, Zenny said, "Thank you. I really needed to know that."

"Soon people should start noticing that things have calmed down. That will help you, when you are ready to tell them what happened to you."

"Thank you Jessica," Zenny said as she hugged her friend.

"I think it's a good idea if you lay low for a while. I'll bring you, your supper and breakfast. That way no one will see you with your hair braided in copper wire, until it is time for you to tell them."

"I really appreciate it," Zenny replied meekly.

Feeling embarrassed and ashamed for having unknowingly caused such distress, havoc, and damage to the compound, especially since they had taken her in and made her feel welcome, didn't sit well with Zenny's conscious.

Jessica left the room and did as she promised. She brought both her dinner and breakfast meals to Zenny's room.

Zenny had not heard from Turris all day. She thought that perhaps, he was spearheading most of the clean-up. So she eased her mind and tried to find solace in Jessica's words.

Chapter Forty-Seven

Zenny knew that calling upon Asher, once-again would be unwise. Instead she turned her thoughts to Emily. *I wonder if she is still up there? Does she hear my pleas?*

There was only one way for Zenny to find out. Trying to speak with Emily didn't come easy. Zenny tried to speak to the moon, but it felt devoid of life, hollow, and empty. Next she spoke out loud.

"Emily, please, I don't know where to turn. I want to do the correct things, but I seem to have made a huge error. I think that during the time when Helena had me under her spell, she didn't allow me to remember what she had done to me. I think that is when she placed her essence inside my hair. I know you're out there somewhere in the Aether, but I just don't know where. Please help me to not cause any more problems for these good people."

It was 4 a.m. when Zenny finally drifted off to sleep.

"You're doing a wonderful job, Zenny. I know you are finding things hard to cope with, but you will soon discover that it is making you stronger. You are learning how to use your talents. Yet, in learning about your abilities, one also tends to fall back on old habits. This can cause them to not understand that things are not always easy. For now, sleep well Sweet pea, for tomorrow will bring a new day."

Zenny woke to Jessica's knocking upon the door. Opening it wide enough for her to enter and bring in the tray of food, Zenny quickly closed it behind her.

Sitting down to eat her breakfast, Zenny said, "Has Turris been asking for me?"

Jessica hesitated for a moment then said, "Yes, and he wondered why he couldn't call upon you." In a hushed toned she added, "I told him, you were still tired from you time with Helena and that you needed to sleep. He didn't seem to appreciate that answer, but he didn't ask about you again." Looking around the sparse room, she added, "I'm certain he will want to see you today to reassure himself, that you're fine."

A quick pursed smile crossed Zenny's lips as she responded, "I think Emily came to me last night in a dream."

Zenny waited and tried to judge Jessica's reaction to the dream. As Zenny waited for Jessica's response, she realized that she was doing what she had done before. She wasn't allowing her abilities to find the answer, instead she fell back into her old habits of trying to guess how a person felt.

Beginning to understand more of Emily's words from last night, Zenny smiled to herself.

Jessica noticed the smile on her face and said, "Did she make you happy?"

Looking at Jessica with bewilderment, Zenny questioned, "Why would you ask that?"

Jessica replied with a slight grin on her youthful face, "You were smiling."

With a nod of her head, Zenny realized that Jessica was fine knowing that she communicated with Emily. Zenny began, "I spoke to her before I went to bed, in hopes that she would talk to me, but she didn't. Then I had a dream that she reassured that I'm doing the things that I should be doing ... but she added that I will probably experience more setbacks in order to help me learn, what my capabilities are." Giving a terse smile, Zenny added, "I didn't really like that part, but I know that what she said is true. I just wish that I would have known all of this long ago, so I would have been able to work on it when I was a child."

Looking wistfully, Jessica responded, "I wish I had your abilities." Rising from the small table, which they were sitting at. Jessica picked up the trays, she said, "Will you be telling Turris soon?"

"After you leave here, I will call him on the Viscom and ask him to meet me here," Zenny said with a quiver in her voice.

Placing her free hand on Zenny's shoulder, Jessica said, "Everything will be fine. Nothing has happened since the fire. That should help

Turris to understand that since I wove the copper strands into your hair, nothing has happened." After pausing for a brief moment, Jessica added, "The Luminary has been good to you ... to us! I am grateful for his help, just as I am certain others are as well."

"I hope so," Zenny replied as Jessica left the room.

Chapter Forty-Eight

It wasn't long after Jessica's departure, before Zenny heard the communication device sound. Pressing the button for speaker only, Zenny heard Turris's voice on the device.

In a panicky voice Turris said, "Zenny, are you alright?!"

"I'm fine," Zenny responded, as calmly as possible, then added, "I was going to call you in just a few minutes."

Silence, filled the air, the Turris spoke. "Why don't you have your viewer on?" he questioned further.

Without answering his question about the viewer, she said, "I would like for you to come to my room, if that won't be too much of a bother for you."

"I'll be right there," Turris replied and ended the conversation abruptly.

Minutes later, a knock came upon Zenny's door.

"Who is it?" she questioned.

"It's me, Turris."

Walking with shaky legs, Zenny opened the door slowly, then quickly moved behind it, as Turris entered.

"What are you doing behind ... ?"

Turris didn't finish his sentence as Zenny shut the door and stepped into Turris' sight.

Not certain how to respond to Zenny's new hair style, instead he smiled politely and said, almost apologetically, "I didn't know you changed your hair. Is that why you didn't have the viewer on?"

Feeling just a bit of relief, Zenny said, "That's part of the reason."

Zenny then, began to tell Turris about the past couple of days as he seated himself at the small table. Zenny also told Turris what the Luminary had said to her.

Turris listened intently until Zenny was done talking.

Walking over to the woman who looked nearly child-like at the moment. Turris said softly, "You did the right thing. I will tell the compound, what has taken place and that there is no longer anything to fear. But, as you stated, the people who committed the acts, must be attended to. They will need to strengthen their will, if they are going to be able to live here. We cannot have people who are easily manipulated by other people or ... other beings."

Pulling Zenny into his strong, warm embrace, he whispered softly into her ear, as he gently kissed her cheek, "We are *The Sensitives* after all, and we must have control over our own minds."

Nuzzling his face into Zenny's welcoming neck, he kissed her pulse point.

Looking into Turris's lowered face, Zenny kissed his lips, as the two embraced as if they had been apart for many years.

———⬤———

AN HOUR LATER, TURRIS and Zenny left her room. Walking together into the hall, Turris called out to Otto and asked him to gather everyone into the dining hall.

When nearly everyone was assembled, except those who could not attend without disruption to their duties of keeping the village safe, Turris told the compound about what happened. Nearly everyone was reassured. However the newer recruits still didn't have the trust that the older recruits did. The new recruits were hesitant about putting all their faith in these people that they hadn't known for very long. But, most felt somewhat reassured.

Chapter Forty-Nine

As the days wore on and life in the compound began to return to normal, Zenny felt that she would soon be tasked with another assignment.

Drifting off to sleep at night, Zenny would hear voices coming from the world. Seeing disturbing images enter her mind as she her sleep deepened, left Zenny with very uneasy feelings. Something big was going to happen, she could feel it.

One night horrified her to her core. Unable to stop the sights and sounds as she slept, her body was in a sleep paralysis state, which she was unable to awaken herself from. The sounds of screams were chilling and remorseful, haunting and terrifying.

"Time! Help us please!" came the desperate woman's voice as she carried a small child in her arms. The woman ran down the street as blue-beams of light shot down from the sky. Fires were erupting all around her and the child.

Parents began screaming as their children vanished in front of them without any perceivable explanation. Others were running in every direction, as the beams continued their destruction.

Some of the intense blue-beams hit the people, and other beams instantaneously melted huge building into oozing masses of molten metal and plastic. Within moments of the devastation, the oozing rubble of the buildings, began to look as if they were made of melted stone and glass.

Zenny, although she wasn't able to stop the terrifying sounds and images, noticed that things didn't appear to look right. She noticed that while everything around the people, including the people who were burned and melted, none of the trees, plants, or other greenery was touched.

"Please help me to stop this from happening," Zenny said in her dream.

A rose scented voice entered into Zenny's dream saying, "You are doing well. I will try to guide you and the other Sensitives to help the people and Earth to try to stop what might come to pass."

Zenny looked around. She continued to feel, as if, she were lucid dreaming, and yet had full function of her body and words.

"Who are you?" Zenny questioned the scented voice.

"I am Emily."

Stunned silence passed as Zenny allowed the full implications of Emily's presence.

"Emily?" Zenny squeaked out.

"Yes, it is I. You do not need to fear. We know that you have been in contact with Asher. Time is helping him to guide you, but unfortunately," Emily added in a lightly exasperated voice, "Asher still has not learned how to control his patience. I will be here to help guide you, along with Asher. We will do our best to show you how to defeat the Mooncalves." Taking a moment to allow Zenny to feel her words, Emily continued, "The Mooncalves are very deceptive. At one time the lived solely upon the Earth, but now they have made the Moon their home."

Zenny interrupted asking, "I thought you were the Moon. Don't you dwell there anymore?"

"No, I do not. My home is now pure spirit and vibrational light. I am everywhere at all times, so too is Asher. Father Time has tasked a number of us to help save the 'just' beings of the Earth. But, since the Mooncalves have infiltrated every aspect of the human society and made things that were once unthinkable, acceptable, such as; worship of idols, such as movie stars, singers, etecetra and images, such as: bulls, goats, pornography, including horrid acts done to and upon and the children; We, the Spirits of Light, have lost many good Earthly souls to the darkness. They have opted for monetary values over spiritual ones.

The songs, which the musicians sing, are actually spells, being cast upon those who choose to listen to the lyrics. Those who hear the songs, but do not listen, are the souls who choose the goodness over darkness. For they are the ones with open eyes and are not blinded by baubles and man-made possessions of the Earth."

"There's a lot of chaos happening here," Zenny interjected, and continued, "so are you saying that the people who have chosen money, fame, and wealth, are all bad?"

"Not all, but the majority of them are. Some pulled themselves away years ago, others are in the process of leaving, but still others are in the grip of the darkness and choose to have fame and notoriety rather than freedom and peace. Those are the ones who, are actively pursuing as many souls into their depravity as they possibly can.

They need to cause fear and panic to keep their souls fed by the humans of the Earth. They are the ones who have taken numerous children into their clutches and use their bodies to feed upon them when they need replenishing of their darkness. For without the young and innocent, they would dry up and turn into what they truly are.... a vehicle of darkness for the forces of evil.

They are beginning to feel the Earth swallow up the monstrosities which they have become. They see others of their kind being crushed by the good who are constantly at battle with them. But, they also feel that they have a purpose to fulfill before they just roll over and die. They know that the Mooncalves created them for a purpose and that is to serve evil. They are also aware, that they must bring a certain amount of good souls back with them before their bodies expire. If they don't then they will end up for all eternity if the midst of the endless realms of oblivion, never feeling alive, but also never feeling death.

They would spend their time in eternity of putrid death, neither alive nor dead. Or until Time decides to 'try' them for their evil ways and then pass judgment upon them. For some reason, they believe that they can bypass the judgment of Time. But, they don't know the true nature of the 'being'. They only know how to exist in the body of flesh, and not in the spirit. The "Mooncalves" have blinded them with so many luxuries and toys, that they can no longer feel love, joy, or any other emotions except for lust, envy, pride, power, and unquenchable thirst of the young.

"This is very overwhelming," Zenny said.

"I must leave your presence very soon, but I will be back again. Until then, know that the Mooncalves are NOT human and they do not want anything which is good for the people or the Earth. They want to transform the world into their playground of filth and abominations, which they are trying to genetically create."

With those last words, Zenny fell into a deep, and restless sleep.

Chapter Fifty

When morning finally arrived, Zenny awoke with sleepy eyes. She felt unwilling to get out of bed, but knew she had to rise.

Leaving the comfort of her bed, Zenny walked over to the small table in her room and sat down. Placing her face in the palms of her hands, she sighed.

Speaking into the emptiness of the room, she said, "I need to tell Turris what I was told." Continuing to speak into the empty room she added, "I wonder if any Spirit Light has come to him?"

Several minutes later, Zenny left the room.

Walking into the long hall, Zenny saw a new recruit and asked if she had seen Turris.

"No," responded the small woman with thin eyes. "I know that he was supposed to come to the training room and talk with us, earlier this morning, but he didn't show up."

Zenny nodded, and said, "Thank you. I guess I'll have to try to see if he is in his room."

The two women parted.

Walking further into the compound, Zenny went to the dinning hall and decided to call Turris on the communications device.

Pressing the button, Zenny waited for Turris to answer, but there was no response. Not certain what to do next, she decided to see is if she could find Jessica or Otto, perhaps they had seen him today.

An hour later Zenny came upon Otto.

"Hi Otto," Zenny called out to the man as he near her in the hall.

"Hi Zenny. How are you doing? You look good, no matter what anyone says about it," Otto replied and then gave a light smile.

Zenny for just the briefest of moments thought that Otto was being serious, but with the little smile at the end, she realized that he was just teasing her, and she smiled in return.

"Otto, have you seen Turris?" Zenny questioned.

"Not since yesterday," he replied.

Thinking back, Zenny realized that she hadn't see Turris at all yesterday and today she hasn't been able to find him. *"Why didn't he say anything to me about leaving?" she wondered to herself.*

"Where did you see him yesterday? Did he say anything about not being around today?" Continuing her line of questioning, she said, "He was supposed to train some of the new recruits today and didn't show up."

"I don't know how to answer you, Zenny," Otto replied. "Perhaps, if you can't find him in the next hour or two, you could go to the viewing station and see if anyone there, knows where he might be."

"That's a good idea," she replied.

With that Zenny walked away and decided not to wait for another hour or two. Entering the viewing station, Zenny said to the people in the small room with its various views of the outside, "Has anyone her seen Turris today?"

A few of the people turned towards Zenny's direction hearing her question.

A large man with black, tightly-curled hair answered, "he said, that he would be out of the compound today and possible not be back until tomorrow or the next day."

Taken aback, and feeling, as if, she should have been informed of his where abouts, Zenny said, "Will you tell me where he went?"

"I don't know. He just said he had to leave," the man replied simply.

Not having any more answers than she did earlier, Zenny left the viewing room.

For the entire day, Zenny wondered what could have caused Turris' sudden departure, especially since he didn't even let her know that he was leaving. Soon night came and Zenny finally went to her room and drifted off to sleep.

Chapter Fifty-One

"Zenny, help me! I need you," Turris said calling out to her.

"I can't see where you are, Turris. Show me the way and I'll come to you," she replied.

All was silent. Zenny waited to hear Turris speak again, but it didn't happen.

Waking up with a jolt, Zenny knew something was wrong, for Turris was trying to reach her in her sleep. Looking at the small clock next to her bed, the time showed, 3 a.m.

"It's not safe for me to leave the compound at night, alone," she thought to herself. *"It's so early, I don't know if I should wake up Otto to have him come with me."*

Looking around her room, as if, she would find an answer there, she thought to herself, *"What if I'm wrong? What if it's just a dream and he's fine?"*

The rose scented voice of Emily entered the room, as she said, "Go to him."

That was all that Zenny heard, but it was enough for her to take action. Rising swiftly, Zenny dressed and went to the Visvoc and called up Otto.

Otto answered groggily, "Yes."

"Otto, I'm sorry, but I need you to help me," Zenny said with alarm in her voice. "Turris needs our help. I saw him in my dream calling out for me."

Otto perked up. He knew that Zenny was gifted and trusted her dreams and instincts.

"Let's meet at the front hall. I'll be there in ten minutes!" he said, as he ended the conversation.

Ten minutes later, both Zenny and Otto were at the front hall. Zenny had a backpack loosely strapped to her and slung around her shoulder. She had placed various items in the bag, that she thought she might need when coming to the aid of Turris.

"Do you have any idea where we should begin to look for him?" Otto questioned as they proceeded to the flyer.

"I saw an image of a large snake that could crush a man," Zenny replied.

Otto thought for a while and was unable to think of where a snake that large, existed in the present age.

As Otto started the flyer, Zenny said, as she recalled a dream of hers, "The snake was yellow with red dots on its body."

Lifting into the air, Otto was deep in thought, trying to piece together Zenny's dream.

Both sat in silence for a long while, as they drifted silently over the vast desert sand fields below. Nearing the city, Zenny noticed a building with yellow on the exterior. Though it wasn't a snake, it felt as if this is where she was meant to be.

"Otto," Zenny said as the building drew closer, "would you fly over that building? See the one with the light yellow on it?" she said pointing to the building in the distance.

Nodding, Otto flew over the building. Zenny noticed red with yellow tiles on the roof.

"Do you see that Otto?" Zenny questioned.

"Yeah. Let's have a closer look," Otto replied.

Feeling a wave of fear creep into her body, Zenny said, "I think he is in there! What is that building?" she questioned Otto.

"That's the food station, where the government doles out allotments of food for the people in need."

"Didn't that used to be the internment camp?" Zenny questioned.

Otto nodded.

Shaking her head in disbelief, Zenny commented, "Somehow, it just doesn't feel right to be giving out food, from a building that once held prisoners." Looking out the window as they continued on, Zenny added, "I remember that they held people there just because they spoke the truth. I remember that they had held parents that didn't follow the guidelines of the school policies. Some of the parents didn't want their children subjected to the brainwashing and glorifying of sexual acts towards young people." Taking in a shaky deep breath, she continued on, "There were also parents who disagreed with wanting their children exposed to making themselves into an abomination. But, the school board for some reason thought they could have a say over how to raise a child rather than what the parents actually wanted."

Otto listened the words, which Zenny had said and it made him visibly shudder. However, as they neared the building, Zenny's words increased in their speed. He knew that she was trying to keep her emotions under control, so she blurted out, whatever came to her mind. In one way it reassured Otto that they were in the right place, but then again, it made him feel tense knowing that they may be in great danger.

After coming up with a plan, Otto landed on top of an abandoned building that was nearby. Zenny would go to the food station and request food, especially since it was almost 7 a.m. by the time they reached their destination. She would have to show her papers stating that she was in need. So before she could request the food, Otto called the compound and told them to send a forged paper through the viewer, that showed that Zenny was eligible. After the paper came through, Zenny left the flyer.

Calling out to her as she walked away, Otto said, "Be careful."

"I will," Zenny replied and added, "Remember, if I should need you, all I have to do is call from the Visvoc."

Otto smiled with relief.

Chapter Fifty-Two

Easily passing the security at the front door, with her faked paper, Zenny entered the building. Seeing the large line of people waiting for food,[5] pulled at her heart strings, but she knew that at this point, she was unable to help any of them. Focusing her thoughts upon Turris, Zenny walked over to one of the guards and asked where the restroom was.

Looking disapprovingly at her, he said, as he pointed, "Down the hall and to the left." Eyeing her suspiciously, he added, "Don't think we aren't watching you. We have cameras all over this place." Then with one added barb, the man said, "Don't try to steal anything. You people are such low-lives, why don't you get a job and work like the rest of us?"

Seeing the sneer upon the man's face and the total lack of compassion, caused Zenny to bite back a rebuttal. She knew better than to start something, which she couldn't, at this point in time, win.

Smiling and nodding politely, Zenny walked down the hall and turned left, just as the man instructed. Fortunately, this is the direction which she felt she needed to go. Instead of turning towards the restroom, Zenny followed her instincts. She looked around for camera's. They were there, however, they were only for show and didn't actually work.

Thinking to herself, *"Of course they won't work, for this is where prisoner's were held before and they wouldn't want the world to know what was truly going on here."* Looking around a bit more, she thought, *"If they are still doing nefarious things here, then of course, the camera's still won't be working."*

Seeing a sudden image pop into her mind, Zenny saw Turris reaching out to her. She was also able to make out some of his words. They were a bit garbled. It was, as if, they were being blocked by some device.

"I ... here ... will ... wait ... soon!" came the message from Turris.

The building was surprisingly empty. *"So who was holding Turris and why? Why did he come here in the first place?"* Zenny thought.

Zenny came to a room which had a Nehushtan on its door. It looked like a snake coiled around a brass rod. She sensed this was the correct room. Zenny placed her ear to the door, to see if she could hear anyone talking inside. It was quiet. Taking a deep breath she looked inward to herself. Allowing her senses to freely experience the atmosphere inside the room, safety washed over her. The young woman, knew she was able to enter the room.

Though, for a moment, doubt crossed her mind. Taking one last deep breath, Zenny said softy, "trust in yourself." Grasping the doorknob firmly Zenny turned it, and pushed the door open.

In a corner, of the nearly empty room, Zenny saw Turris. He was standing at a table with a device on it. Unable to view his face, for he was facing the wall, she wondered why he just stood there and didn't leave on his own volition. As she cautiously neared, she saw that his hands were firmly strapped to a metal bar which was attached to the wall. The screen behind him, had sounds emanating from it, cycling over and over. It wasn't much of a sound, but it did have a strange effect on Zenny's body as she neared.

Not being able to see Zenny, but feeling her presence, Turris called out softly, "I'm glad you found me." With a heaviness in his voice, he added, "the sounds from the machine are interfering with my ability to send messages."

Zenny saw Turris' head drop.

Rushing over to him, Turris popped his head up again saying, "Don't touch me! I'm strapped to the wall with a short chain, but I am also wired to a floor grate with electricity," his voice trailed off.

Zenny could feel the tiredness in his words. She wanted to grab him and hold him in her arms, but Turris was warning her not to do so. Waiting for him to speak again, Zenny's eyes teared up, but she needed to keep calm, so once again, she breathed in deeply ... waiting.

Turris tried to look over his shoulder, as he said, in a pained voice, "if you touch me, both you and I will feel quite a jolt or possibly worse."

Turris' mind was jumping back and forth due to the sounds emanating from the device.

Though his next words were out of context, Zenny understood the situation.

"I had such difficulty contacting you," the haggard man said feeling a weariness pass over his body. "The interference of the sound is messing with my sending capabilities." Pausing to catch his breath, he added, "I'm really glad you're here."

"I'm glad I found you," Zenny replied in kind. Speaking to the back of the man's head, she continued, "I will figure out a way to release you."

Turris' head dropped again.

Zenny knew the situation was dire, and also time limited, for at any moment someone could walk in. She had so many questions to ask Turris, but now, was not the time to do that. She needed to think of a way to get him out of there before anyone showed up.

"Turris," Zenny said as she took in the metal grate, which he was standing on, "Do you know how often someone comes in here?"

"It appears to be about once an hour," he responded in a fading voice, as he added, "I don't know who they are, but I do know that they work in nine hour shifts, for I hear difference voices. They don't want me to sleep," with a slight laugh, he added, "I don't think it would be to my benefit if I did. I think I would be jolted into alertness, way before my knees would hit the ground."

"That's not funny," Zenny said lightly, as she looked around the room for some sort of device to help her remove Turris from his current situation.

" ... just need a little bit of levity," he replied wearily. "I'm growing quite weak."I wasn't certain if you would make it here in time, but I'm glad you did."

Shaking her head at the man, Zenny looked around the room. She didn't see any viable item for her use in helping remove Turris from his current situation. Opening her backpack, she grabbed out a rope, a police baton, some duct tape, and various other items.

Jury-rigging what she hoped would work, ... she tied the rope to the baton and then duct taped it securely, to make certain it wouldn't come off.

Walking closer to Turris, Zenny tossed the rope and baton over a very strong beam. Watching the baton swinging freely in the air, she said, "I have a baton that I threw over a beam. I'm going to walk over to the baton. I will throw the baton and extra rope over your shoulder. Do you have enough freedom in your hands to grab it?"

He sighed deeply, with weariness, saying, "How do you think that will help me?"

He wasn't trying to be sarcastic, he just didn't understand how it would help.

"I was thinking," Zenny said, with as much conviction as possible, "when you grab it, I would use all my weight and lift you off of the ground pulling you upwards, that way the electricity won't effect you."

Turris, was becoming more weary by the moment. He felt that if he lost his life now, at least he had, had one more moment with the woman he loved. "Do what you can," he replied.

Taking a deep breath in, Zenny said silently, "Emily, Asher, Jacob, please help me now. Please give me the strength to lift him and bring him safely to me." Pausing, she added, "Father Time, please allow me to free Turris."

Zenny tossed the roped baton to Turris, he grabbing it he said, "I have a hold of it."

With fierce determination, Zenny pulled with all her might. Feeling her body lift off the floor she called out to Turris, "Are you lifted up?"

"Yes," he called out.

Taking the free end of the rope, Zenny flung it around a beam, numerous times, so it would not slip when she released her weight from the rope. Hopping the few feet to the ground, Zenny grabbed her back pack and took out bolt cutters. Running over to Turris, she stopped short of the grate, which was only two feet wide. Leaning over with the bolt cutters in hand, she cut through the heavy chain, which took more than one time of trying, but she did it. After getting the final cut in Turris was free of the chain.

Time was of essence now. Zenny and Turris, both knew that the people would soon be arriving to check in on their captor.

Looking at Zenny, Turris said, "Give me a push, so I can swing outward, then I will jump away from the grate onto the ground."

Zenny did as instructed.

Turris jumped onto the ground.

Neither of the two could hardly believe what just happened, and that it actually worked, but now was not the time to ponder the subject. With the briefest of hugs, the two embraced, then quickly went to remove themselves from this place. A renewed sense of vigor passed over the couple. With swiftness, they left the room.

Dodging the few people in the hall wasn't too hard, for they seemed preoccupied in their own thoughts. Finally, they were out of the building.

Seeing Otto in the flyer, they rushed over to it, and entered in. Soon they would be back at the subterranean village and have the safety which it provided.

Chapter Fifty-Three

Otto couldn't believe his eyes, there were Turris and Zenny rushing towards the flyer. Happily he started the vehicle and welcomed them aboard. During the flight, Turris explained why he had a need to go to such a place.

He began, "I was summoned by a voice and I was told that I needed to leave immediately. I was told to come alone. I didn't think about the feeling that came with hearing those words, but if I would have given it much thought, I would have realized that it didn't feel right. I suppose

I should have given it more time," he said meekly, but when voice said it was urgent and to not waste time, I really didn't think of anything else."

Zenny touched Turris' shoulder and said, "I'm just so happy you're safe." Pondering for a moment, Zenny said, quizzically, "I wonder if it was Helena, who sent you that message?"

No one had the answer, so they let the issue drop.

———◉———

FINALLY, THEY WERE back at the encampment. Turris went straight to his room and took a long nap. After awaking, he went to the Viscom. He wanted to call Zenny to speak with her. Zenny didn't answer in her room, so he called Otto. Otto told Turris that she was in the dining hall with Jessica. Turris left his room and went to the hall.

Upon seeing Zenny, he hastened his long strides as he neared her.

Seeing his approach, Zenny stood up and the two embraced.

Zenny said smiling, "You are looking much better than you did earlier."

"I feel well rested," he replied.

With a welcoming wave of her arm, Zenny gestured for Turris to seat himself at the table with her and Jessica.

The three sat together and talked and ate their meals. When night came, they went to their rooms and slept peacefully.

———◉———

AS ZENNY AWOKE FROM her nights slumber, she knew it was time for her to talk to Turris about the lucid dream had shortly before he went missing. She knew that they must help the Earth, for Emily had made it quite clear that there was imminent danger. The Sensitives needed to rid the world of the vileness, which was consuming the people and land.

Around 10 a.m., both Zenny and Turris had some free time to talk.

Turris suggested that they go to his room, so they would be able to speak freely and openly without prying eyes or ears. In time The Sensitives would to be informed about the upcoming events, but for now they had to set a plan in motion, so they would be better at directing each person to the roll or rolls that they would eventually need to play.

As lunch time came, Zenny and Turris left his room. They went into the dining hall looking for Otto and Jessica. They wanted to tell them some of the details of their plan.

After relating all their ideas and the reason for them, Zenny asked Otto and Jessica if they had any input or ideas of their own that she and Turris didn't think of.

Instead of getting input, Zenny saw fear, confusion and terror in their eyes.

Zenny touched Jessica's shoulder and said, "Don't worry, we *will* work this out." Pausing briefly she added, remember, Emily and Asher are available to help us. I don't know when they will come to me again, but I do know it will be very soon."

Jessica finally responded as her thoughts began to clear, "We must stop these things from happening!"

Trying to calm her friend, Zenny moved her hand from Jessica's shoulder, and gently placed it on top of Jessica's hand. Zenny responded softly, "You're right; we will stop these things from happening. That is why I know, I will soon receive some type of instruction in order to continue this fight. I also believe that is why Turris was called to the building."

Otto asked, "What do you mean?"

"At first I thought it might have been Helena, who called him there," Zenny said in thought, then added, "I now think, it was to give us an insight into where we need to be, or at least, who we need to talk to. For we need to find out more information about the hidden passages, which are strewn throughout this realm. Then we will be able to use them to our advantage, along with getting rid of the evil which dwells within the passages."

Turris chimed in saying, "I do recall some of the things the people who took me, were saying to each other." Reaching into his pocket, he pulled out a small notebook, saying, "After having a good nights sleep, back in my own bed, I wrote down things that if felt were important to remember. I didn't know why I thought they were important, but I wrote them down any ways."

"Did you write down anything about tunnels or passage ways?"

"I don't recall any type of tunnel," Turris said, "as he paged through his notes, but I did write down something, about a time and place that the guards were talking about." Taking in a deep inhalation as his body physically shook from remembering the events which so recently occurred, he said, "Thursday at 2 p.m."

The three others looked at each other trying to put that information to use in their minds.

Jessica said out loud, "Do you know which Thursday?"

Paging further into the notebook he read, "October 23rd."

Looking around the room Turris turned his head upwards as images flowed through is mind. *Silence filled his ears as the room enclosed around him, as if in an embrace. A large eruption spewed from the ground and shook the floor with waves of sand flowing across a vast expanse. Hearing screams in the distance, Turris looked to the voices, seeing children fleeing from a cavernous opening in the ground. Numbers crossed over the top of them. 24.178, 14.1227. Moments later flyers were scanning the skies searching for the fleeing children. A deep, large, ceramic bowl of crystal pure water appeared in front of the children, all climbed eagerly into the bowl, allowing relief to take place from the hot, molten rocks which where were spewing all around their small bodies. The waves of sand were swiftly swallowed up, the children were brought into view of the world.*

Turris heard a voice coming from above the water filled bowl, with children in it, "These are the children who have lived in shackles and immense terror all their lives, these are the children who are now named, the 'Prayer Pickers'. You will no longer see these children for they are now the chosen ones who will serve as judges of this putrid world and turn the good into their pure golden light.

They will seal the fate of the bad and evil. They will aid you in finding the 'unjust' for they have lived their lives in the clutches of pure evil. They will help you through your journey. You have done well and your journey is not over.

These pure children are now here to help you finish this task. They will help bring the future to its true light. I must go now, but know this, you and Zenny have one more task at hand. I will talk with you soon."

The voice stopped, all went back to its normal place. Turris looked around the room and saw three sets of eyes staring at him with concern.

Gently laying a hand on his broad shoulder, Zenny questioned, "Are you alright?"

With a befuddled nod of his head, Turris replied, "I just had a deeply disturbing vision. I was told that, you and I, are to have one more task of great importance, and after that the world will have peace, *if* we do our work properly. The 'Prayer Pickers' are coming to pass judgment upon the people and beings of the world. They are beginning to start their trials now. We are to find the Mooncalves and send them off to judgment."

Looking confused, Zenny questioned, as the other two chimed in, at the same moment, *"What are the Prayer Pickers?"*

Turris relayed his images to what he saw and heard. He explained what must be done. The three stared in stunned silence.

Zenny finally said, "I don't understand, does that mean the the world will end after we complete our mission?"

"No," Turris replied, "it means, that we must do our part to rid the Mooncalves from the Earth. We must help assist, the Prayer Pickers."

"Why don't they just do it on their own," Jessica chimed in.

Turris said in a calm, reassuring tone, "It is to prompt us into action. To realize that we are not ruled by others. That we are our own selves with personal autonomy, and freedoms which were given to us by Time."

Turris continued on, the three sat in silence contemplating what he was saying. "They are here to help us find the Mooncalves. We will then flush them out into the open, which will allow the world to see how their evilness has spread upon the Earth.

Most people will be willing open their eyes to the truth. Some of course, will choose to not believe, for they don't want to see how far they had strayed from the truth. The Prayer Pickers will gently try to help those who do not want to see, but they will not force it upon them, for in their own time, they will learn the truth. But, hopefully it will happen before they reach judgment."

With all the information that Turris had given them, they knew that, they must put an end this decay of society, and stop the Mooncalves. Now it was just a matter of time, so the group of four began to lay their plans in action.

Chapter Fifty-Four

Hours later, after the group of four had time to talk and plan, Otto asked, "Were you given any clues when the voice spoke with you?"

"Do you mean where the Mooncalves might be located?" Turris questioned.

"Yea," Otto replied.

"I think that the numbers that I was given, are the coordinates to where we might find the Mooncalves, or at least get some more information as to where they might be," Turris replied.

Looking at his friend, Otto said, "I believe that sounds right. The numbers seem to be latitude and longitude. I'll go to the main room and check out the coordinates."

Turris nodded and Otto left, after giving Jessica a brief hug. Jessica smiled with Otto's embrace.

Addressing her comment to Turris, Jessica questioned, "Is there anything that you would like me to do?"

Turris replied, "I think we should gather a group of ... about eight people in total. I task you with finding the ones who you feel will be the most suited for this endeavor."

"Do you really think I'm the one who should be doing this?" Jessica asked incredulously, feeling inadequate for such a monumental task.

"I think you are the perfect person to do this," Turris responded, and then added, "you know the people here quite well, and most of them respect what you have to say. So, yes! I do believe that you are the *only* person who is qualified for this job."

Blushing as she stood, Jessica said, "Thank you Turris. I didn't realize that you had such confidence in me, especially, since I really didn't belong here in the first place."

Placing a strong hand upon her narrow shoulder, Turris said, "The Luminary's know who is best suited to be in this place, and if you didn't belong here with us, they would never have allowed you to come here in the first place."

Feeling a sense of relief and gratitude, Jessica smiled and proceeded to do what needed to be done.

Zenny and Turris were standing next to each other as Turris said, "As for you, my love, please let me hold you, for a moment. Soon you and I, we be engrossed in what is to come our way and I would like to feel you next to me once again. I feel a sense of overwhelming responsibility pouring through my body at this minute."

Placing a finger upon his lips, Zenny responded, "Let's not think about that right now. Let's both take time for each other before we start this new undertaking. I am certain that Emily, Asher, and Jacob wouldn't mind, for the were once beings just like us. And they too, were in love."

With those last words, Turris and Zenny walked to Turris' room and closed the door. Two hours later, after speaking in hushed tones, with reassuring hugs, and gentle kisses, the two emerged from the room. They both felt refreshed, renewed, and understood their responsibilities with clearer heads.

Chapter Fifty-Five

Three months later, the people and plans were set to go, and were finally put into motion. With it being such a daring adventure and undertaking, not many of the other Sensitives knew the full plan. All knew, that there were times, when things must be kept under wraps, in order to avoid any accidental or intentional exposure of their plans.

So none[6] one felt left out, or excluded from the mission. Many were actually grateful that they weren't having to have the responsibility, for they knew this was of great importance.

As Otto readied the flyer, Jessica came to him. The two embraced hoping that they would see each other again, very soon. But, to Otto he knew that this time, he might come back. This time was the final battle between evil and good. Jessica also knew this information, but she wouldn't let Otto speak about the possibility of his not returning. She wanted to keep only good thoughts. To show Otto just how much she believed in his return, she mentioned the idea of marriage. Otto had been wanting to broach the subject for quite some time, but he never had the nerve to bring it up.

He was bursting with excitement, when Jessica had causally brought the subject up. That was his chance to say, "When I return from this mission .... will you marry me?"

Her swift embrace and loving answer was, "Yes!"

They told Turris and Zenny of their developments, both were very happy for the couple.

In the back of Turris' mind, he was thinking the same thing, for he and Zenny, but he wasn't quite able to ask the question just yet, he wanted to be certain that both Zenny and he returned safely. Zenny had the same thoughts, but kept them to herself, for she too feared that one or both would not return.

Within minutes, two other of the Sensitives showed up and were ready to enter the flyer. Otto would fly the vehicle, Zenny, Turris, Marcone, and Howard would get off at their designated areas. Marone would meet up with Hilda, who was in Egypt waiting for his arrival. Howard would be dropped off on the ship in the Meditarian Sea where his wife had already been stationed and Xybar was waiting for his arrival. Turris and Zenny would meet up with Ohad, a Sensitives who had been living and stationed in Libya for many years and knew the area well. Otto would wait in Egypt under cover until his flying abilities were needed for a speedy return.

All knew that though this was the battle to end all battles, there would still be a lot of tension and chaos. They knew that people would need time for things to settle down, so people would understand that they no longer had to live under the rule of the Mooncalves. That meant setting up other types of guidance for all the people of the world. There would no longer be one ruling governance. People would take care of themselves and live their own lives. No person would be able to "rule" over another.

There would be at least three arbitrators to help guide the people to a peaceful resolution, just as the Doegone tribes had been doing it for centuries. The three, but not more than five arbitrators would only be in their position for no more than one year at a time. Then for the village, city, town, state, or country, or whatever each area wanted to call themselves, but no more than one thousand people would be 'governed' by those three to five arbitrators.

Each person in the area who was over the age of 36 but not older than 72 would have a chance to be the next arbitrator, however each group of arbitrators must have one young and one older arbitrator, if this wasn't possible, then they would need to seek out someone from another area and ask if they would do the task for the year.

Money would be not paper, but that of gold, silver, or other valuable commodity. Or if the town chose, they could also use the barter system.

For now, that is in the future, but not far away.

Chapter Fifty-Six

Within five days the group of seven were in the areas and positions that they needed to be. Darkness had just fallen. By mid-night they began their task. From each post, the group was able to easily communicate with each other through their thoughts. They braced themselves for what was to be one of the hardest ordeals of their lives.

COMMUNICATING WITH his mind, Turris began "Are all of you ready to start?"

Each responded, "Yes."

"Remember," Turris began, "you must hold your positions no matter what ... do you all understand?"

"Yes," came their replies again.

All were standing in their assigned position. Their feet were on top of a mound of soft sand, which had been warmed by the heat of the day.

Placing their left hand upon a solid copper pole that was buried five feet deep and stood three feet high, they affixed their palm to it, with a special adhesive. This ensured that they would be still connected to the pole if anything should happen to them. After the mission was complete, they would apply a reversing agent, which they kept in their pocket.

Earlier, they had decided the best way to achieve their goal, even if they didn't survive while trying to complete the mission, was to affix themselves to the pole. They would still be connected spiritually, for if their body was removed from the Earth plane, their spirit would continue to flow through the copper pole that had the hand affixed to it.

Sending out the initial vibrational wave, the group braced themselves. None really certain what was to come. However, they did know that by sending out the wave, this would invariably send a signal to the Mooncalves and would cause them to know their exact locations. But, this is what they needed to happen, for they needed to put an end to the Mooncalves control of the humans on Earth.

Half an hour had passed, Turris was beginning to wonder why the Mooncalves hadn't shown up yet, so they sent out a second vibrational wave which grew even stronger and caused a buzzing sound to reverberate through the ground. The wave of energy flowed through the Sensitives and into the vast expanse of space.

With a suddenness, the Mooncalves appeared overhead. Turris then realized that they had been there since the first wave. But, the Mooncalves intentionally chose not to expose themselves right away. They wanted the make the Sensitives use their power, thus weakening them. Which would give the Mooncalves an advantage.

In a shout, through his mind Turris said, "Brace yourselves!"

This forewarning, didn't help Hilda, for an intense quiver of fear flowed through her being as hundreds of ships appeared overhead. Hilda felt faint with fear. Her body began to tremble uncontrollably. In her mind she said, "I can't do this!"

All the other Sensitives said telepathically, "We are in this together and together we will stay. We are here!"

This helped Hilda feel less alone, but the fear still gnawed at her thoughts. However, that is exactly what the Mooncalves wanted to happen. They thrive on fear. They thrive on chaos. They do whatever they can to keep people at each others throats, or keep them as divided as possible, thus it ensures the enslavement of their minds and souls.

Within mere moments, swarms of the Mooncalves came bursting towards the Sensitives. Streaks of lightning caused by the ships, flashed through the sky, lighting up the darkness of the sky. This didn't help Hilda, for then she was able to see just how many ships there really were. But, once again, this was a fear tactic. The large ships loomed overhead. Only moments later, loud booms came from the ships, causing the ground to shake. Continuing on with their fear, they created deafening shrieks in the sky. They Sensitives felt sound reverberate through their bodies.

Turris called out, "Stand your ground! They are doing this for intimidation. They cannot control our minds. They want us to be frightened of them."

Since each Sensitive was trying to control their own fear, they didn't hear the soft pleas and cries coming from Hilda, as she stood in the inky blackness all alone.

The Mooncalves latched onto Hilda's fears, as one of the ships dropped down its occupants. Though there were hundreds of Mooncalves being dropped onto the sand below, Hilda didn't fear the mob that came towards her. It was something else that made her body quake with fright. As she watched the thunderous throng of Mooncalves nearing her, at first they didn't seem as if they were something to fear. They appeared normal looking, just like any other human on Earth, except that there were hundreds of them. Hilda even recognized some as politicians, others as movie stars, some even looked like an entertainer for a child's birthday party. For the moment this eased Hilda's fear, but soon she would feel her panic grow. In mere minutes, their true selves began to be shown to Hilda. None of the other Sensitives were experiencing this, for the Mooncalves had blocked it from the other them. So, they had no idea, as to why they suddenly felt a sense of dread and fear flowing steadily from Hilda.

The Mooncalves bodies and faces began glitching, as they neared the terrified Hilda. They allowed their masks to come off and were showing Hilda their true selves, their true nature.

In her mind, she said her good-byes, as the hideous being approached. Some of the Mooncalves took on a reptilian appearance. Some had bat-like arms without the wings. Others had legs that appeared, as if, they were dragon like with, thick thighs, but without the talons. Even others had cloven hooves. Many of them were over seventy feet tall. The monstrosities loomed high into the sky. Long inky black arms reached into the warm loose sand. A loud screech echoed through the desert.

Hilda felt the ground begin to loose it strength. It was, as if, she was standing on quick sand. She began to feel her body being pulled under as her, as her arm was being wrenched out of it socket. Screaming in pain, Hilda passed out.

Though the other six Sensitives, were also, being bombarded with hundreds of Mooncalves, each one trying to fight their own battle, they knew they needed to help Hilda. They Sensitives sent out a tremendous vibrational burst at the beings, knocking them off their misshaped feet. They re-hardened the ground which Hilda stood on and awoke her with their voices.

Pulling herself back up she faced the monstrosities. The young woman felt her body become rejuvenated as she stood her ground.

After that, the Mooncalves were in a heightened state of awareness. They no longer took the easy approach, they knew that these Sensitives were highly developed and must be dealt with using extreme measures.

In unison, the demons let out a loud screeching sound, out of which lightning poured through their voices, creating a peeling of the sky. Filling the night with a darkness so black, that it left the Sensitives with a feeling of heaviness and dread. Though, it was a full moon, the light was no where to be found. The sky, so thick, so black, that it was hard for the Sensitives to breathe.

Giant waves of sand began to undulate and flow over the Sensitives burying them up to their necks with its tiny pebbles. Knocking all of them to the ground.

Zenny screamed out, "Emily please help us!"

At that same moment Turris, called out to Asher and Jacob asking for their help as well.

An enormous down draft of air came pouring in from the Aether above. The burst was so strong it knocked the Moonclaves back, and also, at the same, time removing the sand from the Sensitives. Time after time as the hours progressed through the night, the Sensitives used their abilities to knock back the Mooncalves, but they were relentless in their effort, trying to defeat the Sensitives.

Chapter Fifty-Seven

Hours upon hours, flowed through space and time, as the battle between evil and good waged on. Evil didn't want to release its will upon the good. They didn't want to give up the power that they once had over the entire world of Earth.

However, with so many Sensitives united, and having the help from Emily, Asher, and Jacob, the Mooncalves were beginning to feel its effects.

Evil wanted to continue it's reign upon the land. They wanted to expand their forces of darkness. Hour after hour the onslaught continued. Every Sensitive on Earth felt the pain that the seven other Sensitives were feeling, not as intense, but it was there none-the-less. The regular people on Earth, felt a shifting, at times, it felt good, and people were polite and kind to each other. But then the next moment, the people were at each others throats, one blaming another. Fighting broke out in places, while others stole items from people's homes or stores.

Time after time the Mooncalves hurdled down propulsion's of destructive energy trying to make the Sensitives stop their barrage upon them, but it was to no avail. The seven didn't falter from their mission. Their battle could not be lost, for if they did lose, then the world would turn to darkness until Time decided that He would reset the world and start anew. Time had given the Sensitives, along with Emily, Asher, and Jacob a chance to redeem themselves, and make the world the place it should have been all along.

By morning the majority of the Mooncalves were defeated, however the ones who were in the air ships continued to fight with voracity and were unwilling to give up the fight for the realm.

Day after day the battle raged on, until the fourth day arrived. By that point the Sensitives were wearing thin. Hunger and thirst gnawed at their bodies. That is when Zenny heard a familiar voice.

"It won't be much longer," Emily said to the exhausted woman. "I am here to help." Feeling a warming touch upon her shoulder, Emily continued, "I am here to give you drink. Asher and Jacob are also helping. We are allowed to give you drink. Keep the faith, your battle is nearly won."

With those words, Zenny felt quenched, so too, did the other seven Sensitives. This gave them a renewed since of hope and vigor.

Time after time, another Mooncalf was erased from the Earth. Blow after blow, landed hard on the Mooncalves. The Earth shook, causing earthquakes as the fight wore on. Lighting peeled through the sky. Waters across the world grew and ebbed. Floods though small, crested over vast tracks of land. Landslides, slide through the hillsides, as water, earthquakes, and wind eroded the land.

Suddenly all went quiet. An enormous tornado spanned over the sand where the Sensitives were positioned, sweeping up some of the Mooncalves. Moments later, a light gentle breeze flitted over the land. Silence befell the Earth. The Sensitives looked around, and noticed after the long days and nights of the arduous battle, the Mooncalves were expunged from the face of the Earth.

The Sensitives could see thousands of Mooncalves strewn across the desert sand, as purple blood oozed from the pores in their misshaped bodies. Moments later, they saw light beings swooping down to remove the bodies from the land.

Time had many to judge and He was not happy with the things that the Mooncalves had done to the Earth, but in time, the Mooncalves will have their say, and Time will judge them accordingly.

Chapter Fifty-Eight

Turris called Otto on the communications device and told him they were ready to be picked up.

Hearing him his name being called on the device, Otto let out an audible sigh. He heard, Turris say weakly into the communications device, "Come and get us. Get Hilda first, then go in order to the others."

"Will do!" Otto answered joyously, relieved that the battle was finally over.

Otto started the flyer and began to pick up his passengers. Each of the Sensitives who were once glued to the pole, had now freed their hand with the reversal agent, elated to be relived of the burden of the pole and task that had went along with it.

Hours later all the Sensitives were picked up and were safely in the flyer.

SHOUTS OF JOY COULD be heard in various parts of the world. But, many people were standing around looking quizzically, at the suddenly silent streets, not understanding what had just happened. Those were the people who Turris and Zenny knew would have problems adjusting to the peaceful Earth. Those were the people who would still want their old lives back. They are the ones who wanted to have all their luxuries and keep their sedentary life style, and the only price they had to pay for all of it was their *freedom*.

They didn't want to work for their food, clothing, or shelter, they wanted it handed out to them by the government. They didn't care what type of binds, or personal information the government had on them, they didn't care that the government spied on their every move, and listened to their every word, knowing that it would eventually be used against them. They *just* didn't care; they wanted their hand-outs and didn't care how high of a price they had to pay.

AS THE GROUP FLEW BACK to the subterranean hideout, they breathed a collected sigh of relief. It had been a very trying few days. Grateful they were returning to their temporary home, they knew that as time passed, the hidden village would no longer have to be hidden. But, until complete peace was achieved, they would have to keep their where-a-bouts secret. For now, however, they were very relieved to be back.

After a decent meal, hot baths or showers, and a good night's rest, all felt refreshed and ready to take on the new day, the new world.

Though they were back in their own regions, each knew they had a long, hard struggle ahead of them. Things needed to be set in motion. They knew there would be a lot of rearranging in the government. People needed to be told what just transpired and why.

People needed to know that they would have to become self sufficient, and empower them to live their new free, and wonderful lives.

With the guidance of Emily, Asher, and Jacob, and with Zenny and Turris as co-pilots, they knew they could and would do it. It will take time, but it will be done. They knew there would be some skirmishes to come and small disputes, but it would never compare to what they had just been through.

They knew there would be push-back, when it came to the people who wanted to do nothing with their lives. But, in time, they would find their way, even it were read a story or tell a story to children. Help people crossing streets. Whatever they could do to help society, is all that would be asked of them, even if it felt mundane or inconsequential. It was for the betterment of the Earth, and that is what matters.

The End ... or is it just the beginning?

Also by D.A. Riles

The House of Here
The Sensitives

Standalone
The Monster We Call Dad
The House of Here

www.ingramcontent.com/pod-product-compliance
Ingram Content Group UK Ltd.
Pitfield, Milton Keynes, MK11 3LW, UK
UKHW040902240225
455493UK00001B/144